MW01136152

"Every new writer has a *Rise of the Spider Goddess* inside them. Now it's been published, there's no need to write it. Chock-full of essential advice, self-mockery, and compassion for the beginner, it's a hilarious reminder that we all start somewhere."

–Sean Williams, author of *The Slug in the Sky* (age 15) and the #1 NYT Bestseller *Star Wars: The Force Unleashed* (age 39)

"There are things you wish you could un-see, like walking in on your parents in the bedroom. There are also books you wish you could un-read, like *Rise of the Spider Goddess*. Most of wish our unpublished work would just stay buried forever, but Jim's novel appears to be undead. Lacking a red pen to kill it forever, we at least have Jim's lively, hysterical, and snarky self-commentary to make the journey worthwhile!"

–Stephen Leigh, author of *The Best Friends Go Diving* (age 12) and *Immortal Muse* (age 63)

"If the Bulwer-Lytton contest gave prizes for whole books, this one would win by a mile. *Eye of Argon* look out! The Spider Goddess is about to steal your crown."

-Diana Pharaoh Francis, author of *City of Terrible Night* (age 16), and *Trace of Magic* (age 47)

"Oh my. I remember all too well my misspent youth in worlds much like this one. This book makes me feel young again. It's magic."

–Alma Alexander, author of *Children of Legend* (age 14) and *Random* (age 51)

"We often learn more from the mistakes of others than from their successes. Hines has been kind enough to put his own errors on display as an object lesson for the student writer: everything from cliches of prose to morally dubious characterization, from paper-thin worldbuilding to continuity errors big enough to fly a dragon through. If you want to know what not to do, read this book."

   –Marie Brennan, author of *World of the Elementals* (age 10) and *Voyage of the Basilisk* (age 33)

"Fans of Jim C. Hines' delightful novels, or his Hugo-award-winning blog will love this annotated edition of Jim's first novel (often referred to as a 'trunk novel' because it should be locked in the trunk of a car which is about to be shoved off a pier into the bay, there to be forgotten until the end of time). Jim's commentary is often laugh-out-loud funny, while the text of the novel suggests the character concerns which shine through in his later work. Whether you are seeking to peer into the mind and process of the author or simply looking for a fun read, this book is for you!"

   –Elaine Isaak, author of *Through Eyes of Fire* (age 16) and *The Singer's Crown* (age 32)

"Publication of this ground-breaking work will no doubt vault its author into the very pinnacle of the genre, thus making his blurb on my next book all the more valuable. (Note: the author of this blurb received no compensation for providing it, nor, of course, would ever dream of asking for such — indeed, the pleasure of reading the work is {nearly} sufficient compensation in itself, and I am duly grateful to Jim C. Hines for this opportunity.)"

   –E. C. Ambrose, author of *Dragonfall*, (a ripoff an homage to Anne McCaffrey, age 12) and the *Dark Apostle* series (age 39)

THE PROSEKILLER CHRONICLES

RISE OF THE

SPIDER GODDESS

AN ANNOTATED NOVEL

JIM C. HINES

This is a work of fiction. Bad fiction. Any resemblance to real persons, living or dead, is both coincidental and highly unfortunate for those persons.

RISE OF THE SPIDER GODDESS

Copyright © 2014 Jim C. Hines

Cover art copyright © 2014 by Patrick McEvoy, www.megaflowgraphics.com

ISBN-13: 978-1502451903
ISBN-10: 1502451905

First Printing: December 2014

Those numbers below? They're normally used to track the print run, which is pretty pointless with a print-on-demand title. So I'm using them to track any significant changes to the text. The rightmost number is the edition number you're holding.

0 9 8 7 6 5 4 3 2 1

I should probably dedicate this to my college D&D group: Rob, Glenys, Edric, Erin, and Jay. But I'm not sure they'd appreciate it...

AUTHOR'S NOTE

DEAREST READER,
The book you're about to read is bad. Bad like waking up at two in the morning because your cat or dog is making that distinctive hacking noise. Bad like your almost-potty-trained child walking out of the bathroom to announce, "I did finger-painting, Daddy!"

I should know. I wrote it.

I've been writing for almost twenty years now, with nine books in print from a major publisher and fifty short stories in various magazines and anthologies, but this book here is where it all began. This is the first book I ever finished, more than a decade before my official debut fantasy novel *Goblin Quest* was released. I wrote this one during my sophomore year in college, based on my then-favorite Dungeons and Dragons character, Nakor the Purple. A D&D character I had created based on Raymond Feist's Riftwar books, making it doubly unoriginal.

There's also a young thief, a pair of pixies, an evil goddess, assorted Bad Guys, and an angsty vampire. Remember, this was written in 1995. I was writing angsty vampires…badly…before it was cool!

For two decades, I did everything in my power to pretend this book never existed. So why did I change my mind now? There are three reasons:

1. I read an excerpt of this book— while dressed as Nakor, no less — as part of a fundraiser. You can learn more about that and see the video at jimchines.com/2013/01/reading-my-very-first-story, if you dare. Some people said they were curious and wanted to know what happened next. Personally, I think there's something seriously wrong with those people, but who am I to judge?

2. I'm hoping this book could serve as a tool to help other writers learn what *not* to do. I know I've learned a great deal over the years by reading not-so-great stories, and I happen to believe this is one of the not-so-greatest. I've annotated the book to point out some of my mistakes, or just to make smart-ass comments.

> Those annotations will look like this.

Don't worry, I left plenty of other problems for you to find on your own.

3. But the biggest reason is that I thought giving my own book the Mystery Science Theater treatment sounded like a lot of fun!

Despite strong, painful temptation, I haven't changed a single typo or poor word choice. If nothing else, I hope this book gives you a laugh. Beyond that, all I can say is that I'm sorry.

Jim C. Hines
October 2014

PS, I really did get better...

"Time, as we understand it, is an illusion. It is not a line, but an intricate web in which all events are interlaced. Creation and destruction — they are one and the same."

    –Taken from the Journal of Averlon Lan'thar

> Every book should open with a pretentious-sounding and utterly meaningless quote from a character we know nothing about. Also, when I rule the world, I'm going to make gratuitous apostrophe abuse punishable by Taser.

CHAPTER ONE

THE CLOUDS SEEMED TO GLOW WITH AN INNER light as the sun began to disappear behind the mountains to the west. Brilliant orange clouds hovered over the dark silhouette of the trees in the distance. In the east, the sky was darker. A few stars were beginning to appear in the sky.

The forest was full of noise. The sound of leaves rustling against themselves blended with the rattling beat of a woodpecker hunting for food. Nearby, the gentle murmuring of a river added its contribution to the symphony of nature. There was a quiet chirping noise, followed by a splash.

Nakor glanced sharply toward the river. On the bank, a raccoon sat happily washing its dinner in the water. With a smile, Nakor turned back and continued to watch the sun set.

They say you should open your story with something interesting to hook your reader's attention.

> You know, like some dude named after a Ray Feist character watching a sunset in the woods. With a random raccoon.

The wind blew his long blond hair away from his face, revealing pointed elvish ears. Clear, pure blue eyes watched contentedly as the sun continued to sink behind the horizon.

> We hope those eyes are, in fact, Nakor's, but you never know. This is fantasy, after all.

Currently, Nakor sat neatly in the top branches of an ancient cedar tree. Over a year ago, he had discovered that it afforded him a spectacular view of the sunset. Ever since, he had climbed this tree as often as possible to watch the sun go down at the end of the day.

The last thing he was expecting was for the tree to speak to him. "Excuse me," came a voice from directly behind him, "but just what do you think you're doing up here?"

Nakor turned and glanced around. There was nobody there, of course.

"What was that?" he asked, confused.

> Totally true fact that I'm not making up: if you took out all the unnecessary adverbs and adjectives, you'd lose approximately 60% of the book.

"What are you doing in my branches?"

He stood up and looked for the source of the voice. Holding another branch for support, he peered around to the other side of the tree. Still, there was nobody.

"Who are you?" Nakor asked curiously.

"Well that's a brilliant question. Who do you think I am?"

He stared at the tree, raising an eyebrow. Still clutching a branch in one hand, he turned to squarely face the tree.

Then a piece of bark slipped beneath his foot.

> Raised eyebrow count: 1
>
> What we have here is the first real bit of danger or tension, which came about...because the protagonist slipped on a piece of bark. Riveting stuff, eh? Wait until you read the scene in chapter four where Nakor trips over a rock!

Nakor's grip failed as he fell from his perch, and he began to plummet to the earth, nearly a hundred feet below.

Closing his eyes, Nakor reached within himself to gather his magical energy. Wincing as he crashed through the small branches, he focussed that energy outward at the air beneath him.

His fall began to slow as Nakor continued to concentrate. A few moments later, he stopped, supported by a cushion of air. Reaching out with one hand, Nakor grabbed a branch and pulled himself closer to the tree. As he slipped off of the magical cushion he had created, he pulled himself up onto a sturdy limb and allowed his spell to end.

Once he reached the branch and was sitting securely, Nakor looked at the tree. "Well that was rude," he muttered.

> Oh, sure. Blame the tree. He's as bad as that one uncle who's always passing gas and blaming it on the dog.

Far above, Whoo looked down at Nakor and giggled. Whoo was a pixie, whose large moth-like wings allowed him to hover high in the air while he watched Nakor in amusement. With a height of about three feet, Whoo was tall for a pixie. He looked a little bit like an elf, with narrow pointed ears and thin tapering eyebrows. Pure silver hair brushed his shoulders as Whoo hovered, grinning in amusement. Pale, colorless hair was a species trait, Whoo was young for a pixie.

With a grin, he flew down to hover next to Nakor. "You looked kind of silly, falling and flailing about like that," Whoo said. Nakor looked for the source of the voice, but could see nothing.

> Being able to shift point of view is a good thing. Bouncing back and forth like Sonic the Hedgehog on a trampoline? Not so much.

Many had described pixies as having the power to become invisible. That was not completely accurate. Pixies could not achieve true invisibility, but they were able to come close. They possessed the ability to make themselves unnoticeable, so that even people who look directly at them would see nothing. It was this talent Whoo was exercising tonight to amuse himself.

> Dear 1995 Jim:
>
> I'm shipping you a year's supply of contractions. Please use them.
>
> Sincerely,
> 2014 Jim

Deciding that perhaps it would be safer to continue this conversation from the ground, Nakor quickly climbed the rest of the way down. As his feet hit the earth, he began muttering another spell. He finished his incantation, and felt a brief chill come over his eyes as they adapted to the spell. This was a simple, common spell taught to most wizards and magicians when they began to learn about spellcasting. It enabled the caster to see the presence of other magic in the immediate vicinity.

Whoo flew lower, and asked "What's the matter now, don't you like my branches?" Whoo liked this game. It was so much fun to confuse the big people. They tended to be so slow.

Nakor grinned. There was a green glowing form floating in front of him, and the voice was coming from the glow. Obviously, somebody was playing a trick on him. Nakor liked tricks. Admittedly, had he fallen the rest of the way, it might not have been so amusing. Nakor decided he wanted to talk to this person, whoever or whatever it was.

The green glow was hovering about a foot off of the ground now. Nakor slipped a hand into a pouch on the back of his belt. "It's not the branches, it's the falling," he said to the tree. Then, he pulled a bola from the pouch, and flung it at the form.

The weighted leather cords wrapped themselves around Whoo, entangling his wings and sending him crashing to the ground. This was definitely unfair. Whoo didn't like this game anymore.

Far above, Pynne sighed to herself. Whoo was fun, but tended to get into trouble if left unsupervised. "Men," she muttered. Flapping her wings, she moved into the open and concentrated, preparing to start her own type of fun.

> To those of you who've read *Goblin Hero*, yes, this is where the character of Pynne originated.

Pixie magicians were rare, but not unheard of. Pynne was one such rarity. She had been an illusionist for years. As she cast her spell, the ancient cedar shimmered briefly, and began to move. A branch reached out to tap Nakor on the shoulder. As Nakor jumped, Pynne smiled to herself. She liked her illusions.

Nakor leapt back, drawing his rapier. He had assumed that whoever was trapped within his bola was the cause for all this mischief. Perhaps he was mistaken.

Whoo struggled to free himself. The bola had tangled itself tightly around his arms and wings. This was going to take some time. Whoo had a sudden thought. Maybe this wouldn't take much time at all. He closed his eyes.

Pynne concentrated. A large face appeared on the tree. The eyes turned to look at Nakor, and the mouth moved as it spoke. "What is it about you people? Do you think you're some kind of bird or something? Next thing I know, you'll be making a nest in my branches, sitting on your eggs."

Nakor frowned slightly. The entire tree was glowing green now. There was a slight rippling effect that seemed familiar somehow. He found himself unable to remember what type of magic would create such a rippling, though. Nakor lowered his sword.

Whoo opened his eyes. The other power that pixies possessed was the ability to change their shape. While it took a great deal of time and energy, they could assume the form of other animals. As a small rat, Whoo had no problem in crawling out from within Nakor's bola. Once free, he began to change back to his regular form.

> It's a useful and potentially powerful skill, one which I completely forgot about after this first chapter.

Pynne was hovering about twenty feet in the air, manipulating her illusion. Consequently, she was the first to see the party of twelve figures approaching. In the lead was a man dressed in an enveloping black cloak. An elf, she decided, judging by the grace with which he moved through the woods. Curious, she dropped her spell and watched.

"Nakor!" called the black robed elf. Behind him, his armed companions began to spread out, surrounding him.

> I'm pretty sure I meant they were surrounding Nakor, not Black Robe, but I'm not 100% sure.

Backing up against the now normal tree, Nakor again raised his weapon. He didn't recognize the men, but he did recognize the cloak worn by the lead elf. That, with the small silver amulet around his neck, marked him as a priest of the spider goddess.

Glancing at the men who were beginning to surround him, Nakor cursed. This was not going to be easy.

With a mental sigh, he reached inside his cloak and pulled out a small glass flask. The priest gestured at the others to halt, unsure of what Nakor was doing.

> "Our enemy is doing something! Quick everyone, let's all stand here to find out what it is!"

Suddenly, Nakor hurled the small flask at the priest. He was too slow to move out of the way, and the vial shattered on his forehead.

The priest paused, confused by the liquid that dripped down his face and neck. It didn't seem harmful, he concluded. Perhaps Nakor grabbed the wrong vial. He looked up.

"Sorry," Nakor said with a smile. One of the first tricks he had ever learned was the ability to create a small ball of fire. He concentrated, focussing his energy into his left hand. A moment later, a small flame appeared there. The spell also protected him from being burnt by the flame.

> "Can we attack Nakor yet?"
>
> "He won initiative fair and square. Don't worry, it should be our turn soon."

The priest's eyes widened as Nakor threw the small flame at him. He ducked to one side and it flew by his head, brushing his shoulder on the way by. Then he screamed as his shoulders and hair began burning.

Nakor flinched at the sound. He hated inflicting pain, even when it was the only way to survive. He also hated wasting the flask of lamp oil, as it was his last one.

Soon, the priest fell to the ground, dead. Nakor waved

his hand, and the flames died out.

"Are you sure you want to do this?" he asked the remaining men, eyeing the dead elf.

One of them stepped forward, wielding an enormous broadsword. "He's mine," the man said viciously.

Nakor studied him, noting the leather breastplate and matching bracers on his wrist. He examined the huge blade of the man's sword, comparing it to his own narrow rapier.

> I was aiming for an, "It's not the size that counts" joke here. I missed.

Nakor ducked under the first swing, shoving his own sword forward to counterattack. The blade skidded off of the leather breastplate, and the man growled.

"Uh oh," Nakor muttered.

With a loud cry, the man pulled his sword back and lunged at Nakor.

Anticipating the move, Nakor stepped neatly to one side. The man grunted as his sword plunged into the tree Nakor had been standing in front of. He began to wrench his weapon free, when a sword blade rapped sharply across his knuckles.

> Probably Nakor's sword blade, but once again, we don't want to make assumptions.

Shaking his head, Nakor gestured at the man to back away. Screaming a battle cry, the man charged.

Nakor dodged to one side, sliding the tip of his rapier up under the man's arm, a place left unguarded by the leather armor he wore. Giving a final, gurgling cry, the man tumbled to the ground.

"That's two," Nakor commented, backing toward the tree. "I'm willing to call it even if you are."

The remaining fighters looked at each other, then began advancing toward him.

"I was afraid of this," he muttered.

The advancing warriors stopped in confusion. Nakor raised an eyebrow, then looked to one side. There, a second Nakor stood, sword in hand.

> Raised eyebrow count: 2

"Shall we?" the new Nakor asked.

With a shrug, Nakor lunged forward, a move that was instantly imitated by his doppleganger. Unsure of what sword to parry, their target died swiftly as a pair of rapiers pierced his body.

Pynne grinned, concentrating on the fighting below. She raised her other hand, and a third Nakor appeared next to the first two. She had always disapproved of unfair fights. This "Nakor" seemed to be a decent enough fellow, and it would be sad to see him killed at twelve to one odds.

Again in his normal form, Whoo looked over to appraise the situation. Glancing up at Pynne, he pointed at the illusions and raised an eyebrow. Pynne smiled innocently.

> Raised eyebrow count: 3

Carefully, Whoo pulled a two foot bow off of one shoulder. Moving with the smooth grace of experience, he slipped the string onto the bow and pulled an arrow from his quiver.

Pixies didn't hunt for food, but they still needed to know the arts of war in order to defend themselves. Whoo was an archer. He had been practicing his craft for over a decade, and was counted as the finest shot in his village. The bow he wielded was painstakingly made by his own hand, as was the arrow he placed gently against the string.

> Why does the author keep interrupting the action to take an infodump?

Completely serious now, he pulled the string back and sighted along the narrow point of his arrow. Relaxing his fingers, he allowed the string to slip out of his grasp.

The three Nakors were holding the mercenaries at bay, but were unable to launch an offensive of their own. Keeping their backs to each other, they parried their opponents' attacks as well as they could.

> Whoo's arrow must be taking the scenic route to its target.

Seeing an opening, one of the men raised his own sword to strike. There was a sharp jolt to his hand, and he looked in shock as his weapon flew away to land point down in the dirt. His hand bled from a small cut where Whoo's arrow had sliced his thumb in passing.

A rapier took him in the throat. It was one of Pynne's illusions, but the man didn't know that. He clutched his throat in agony, eyes widening, and fell to the ground unconscious.

Moments later, another man stumbled to the ground. There he moaned and clutched his thigh, from which another of Whoo's arrows protruded.

"Seven left," Nakor observed.

"No problem," commented the double on his left.

Raising their swords, they prepared for the next assault.

From a nearby doorway, Galadrion watched the last rays of the sun as they faded from view. Careful to avoid stepping into that light, she waited as the last of the sun's light disappeared, spreading a gentle darkness across the land.

> Galadrion's name was totally not stolen from *Lord of the Rings*. It's 100% original, just like the rest of this book!

Sprinting, Galadrion raced toward the sound of fighting

in the distance. Seeing the struggling figures ahead, she slowed to a walk.

One of the combatants turned, hearing her approach. His eyes widened as he studied the woman who stood before him. Galadrion was an attractive woman. She was tall for a woman, with long brown hair. She was dressed in a black leather vest over a white shirt, and black trousers. A leather-bound sword handle jutted over one shoulder.

Puffing out his chest, the man raised a hand, signalling her to halt. "I'm sorry m'lady," he said in an official sounding voice, "we need you to stay clear of the area."

Galadrion didn't reply. She simply reached out and grabbed the man by his neck. There was a snapping sound as her fingers tightened, and she hurled the lifeless body into a nearby tree.

A few of the remaining fighters spun to face this new attack. Galadrion watched impassively as one of them slashed at her neck. At the last moment, she raised an arm and caught the blade in one hand.

"Run," she whispered. Wrenching the sword away, she grabbed the handle in her other hand. With a slight flexing of her muscles, she snapped the blade.

The man's eyes widened, and he turned to flee. His companion watched in disgust.

"Coward," he muttered, raising his own sword.

Galadrion shook her head sadly as she drew her own weapon. Wielding the graceful, curved scimitar with both hands, she waited.

The man brought his sword down in a powerful overhead blow, which Galadrion parried effortlessly. Before her opponent could react, she sliced deep into his side, severing the iron links of his mail armor.

The fleeing man stumbled to the ground, an arrow in his calf.

Galadrion looked in surprise, wondering where the arrow had come from. Turning toward Nakor, she allowed herself a slight smile.

There was only one man left standing, and he was panicking. The three Nakors in front of him smiled in amusement.

Giving a silent prayer, the man lunged at one of the images before him. It gave no resistance, and vanished as his sword touched it. Stumbling, the man turned and looked at the two remaining figures, both with rapiers ready.

Slightly more confident now, he thrust his sword at the image directly in front of him.

Shifting his weight, Nakor allowed the thrust to pass harmlessly by, at the same time extending his own sword. The man tried desperately to stop, but was unable to halt his forward momentum. His face twisted into an expression of pain as he impaled himself on Nakor's waiting blade.

The other illusion vanished as Nakor withdrew his sword from the body. Kneeling down, he wiped the blade clean on the dead man's shirt.

With a sigh, he looked to the west, where the sky was fading into darkness. It had been such a beautiful sunset.

> Connecting the end back to the beginning like this can be a useful and effective technique… unless your beginning was really, really boring.

CHAPTER TWO

GALADRION WALKED OVER TO NAKOR AS HE FINISHED cleaning his rapier. "Are you okay?" she asked.

"Yes."

She nodded curtly, then turned and walked to the unconscious man who had been stabbed by Nakor's illusionary double. She bent over and grabbed him by his cloak. Standing effortlessly, she tossed him over her shoulder like a sack of potatoes.

"What are you doing?" Nakor called out.

Galadrion stopped for a moment. "I'm a vampire," she replied without turning. "You don't want to know."

Nakor watched her walk away. Then he turned around. His spell was starting to wear off, but he could still make out the dimly glowing forms of Whoo and Pynne. "Thank you, whoever you are," he said to the two shapes.

Whoo hesitated briefly, then allowed himself to become visible. Pynne followed suit a moment later, and was the first to speak.

"Interesting friends you have," she said with a wry smile.

"Yeah," Whoo added, "I'm sorry I had to shoot them."

Nakor grinned. Pixies were distantly related to elves, as could be seen by their pointed ears and narrow features. Their language was an offshoot of elvish.

"So you were the ones playing games with me?" Nakor asked, switching to their language.

The two pixies looked at each other, and both started giggling. Pynne was the first to speak. "You have a human accent," she complained.

> The elf-with-a-human-accent thing is actually a deliberate character trait, not a lazy author screw-up.

"I'm Whoo, that's Pynne," the other pixie added.

"You're Nakor, I assume?" Pynne asked.

He grinned. Still speaking in the pixie tongue, he said "That's correct."

Nakor looked around the rapidly darkening woods. "Why don't we continue this discussion at my home?" he asked.

Pynne and Whoo glanced at each other, and shrugged.

"Sure," Pynne decided.

"There's a ruined castle about a quarter of a mile in that direction, by the river. I'll meet you there in a few minutes, okay?"

"What are you going to be doing?" demanded Whoo.

Nakor glanced around at the corpses who littered the ground. "I have to clean up my forest," he answered. I also have to check on a friend, he added silently.

The diminutive pair looked at each other and vanished. Nakor could faintly make out their laughter as they flew toward his home.

Galadrion trembled. The unconscious man lay in a crumpled heap a few feet away, where she had dropped him. She had been a vampire for twenty six years. For twenty six years she had tried desperately to fight the urges, the overwhelming instincts within herself. For twenty six years, she had failed.

> Galadrion is TRAGIC and DARK and TOR-MENTED!

It had been many days since she tasted fresh blood. She slammed her fist into a tree, hating what she was about to do. Bark splintered around her fist, falling unnoticed to the earth. It was a curse, she thought angrily, running her tongue across the pointed tips of her two elongated teeth.

> TRAGIC and DARK and TORMENTED and also CURSED!

She walked back to the fallen man. His forehead was bleeding slightly from when Galadrion had dropped him. She stared, fascinated, at the red drops that gradually ran down the side of his face to drip onto the earth. With a trembling hand, Galadrion reached out and wiped the small cut with her finger.

Galadrion seemed dazed as she stared at the red stain on the tip of her index finger. She studied it for a moment, turning her hand slightly. She could feel her willpower beginning to fail. Screaming silently at herself, she brought her finger up to her mouth and licked the blood.

As the coppery taste hit her tongue, Galadrion finally lost control. She grabbed the body and slammed him viciously into a tree. Shoving his head to one side, she sunk her teeth into his neck and began to drink.

A few minutes later, she tossed the body to one side. She knew that in a few days, the man would awaken a vampire, just as she herself had awoke all those years ago.

It had been the day after her nineteenth birthday. Her husband had come home after a long hunting trip, bringing a stranger with him. He had been pale and sick, and spent the next few days in bed.

The stranger had helped around the house, making himself useful in whatever way he could. The day after he arrived, he walked up behind Galadrion while she prepared lunch. Without warning, he pinned her arms at her side and sank his teeth into her neck.

> "This is *not* making yourself useful!"

Devin, her husband, stumbled into the kitchen upon hearing her scream.

"No!" he protested, grabbing the stranger by the shoulder. "You promised not to take her!"

"Fool," the stranger hissed, dropping Galadrion to the ground. "I give you immortality, and you dare to question my actions?"

> The stranger is also a habitual puppy-kicker, just in case his EVILNESS is too subtle.

Devin pulled a hunting knife from his belt and lunged at the stranger.

He laughed as the knife danced harmlessly off of his skin. His hand shot out and grasped Devin by the throat. Lifting him off of the ground, the stranger carried him out of the house.

A few minutes later, he returned.

> Let's review the timeline. Devin and the stranger arrive at home. Devin, "spent the next few days in bed." But the stranger attacked Galadrion "the day after he arrived," at which point Devin went and got himself killed right out of the story. Um...

"Let this be a lesson to you," he said, kneeling down before the barely conscious Galadrion. "Never challenge another vampire before you have tasted your first blood. Until that time, you are still vulnerable."

The stranger's cruel smile was the last thing Galadrion saw as she lost consciousness.

It was only two weeks later that Galadrion killed for the first time in her life. Whatever she had become had created an insatiable need inside her. The more she fought that need, the more desperate she became for blood. Finally, she raced out of the house and grabbed the first person she could find. Dragging them off into the shadows, she murdered him and drank his blood.

It was odd, she never even saw the man's face. Her only memory of the event was of breaking her victim's neck in an attempt to prevent him from acquiring the curse that had taken over her life. On that day, she had vowed never to do to another person what had been done to her.

Galadrion stood the body against the tree and drew her sword. With one swift stroke, she struck his head from his body. Having done this, she dropped her sword and collapsed against to the ground, hugging her knees.

> We're done with the flashback and back in the present story now. I mention this only because the author didn't think to provide any sort of transition here. Lazy bum.

Nakor watched the beheading from the shadows. He waited calmly as Galadrion sat against the tree, trembling. After a few moments, he stepped toward her.

She heard the footsteps, and knew without looking who it was. Nakor was the only one she knew who could get this close to her without her hearing. With a sudden rush of shame, she remembered her appearance. Blood stained her teeth red and was in the process of drying to a dark crust around her mouth. She was covered in sweat and still trembling from her recent ordeal. Only twice in her life had

Galadrion been found like this. Both times, people had been horrified. They had cursed her, calling her a demon or worse. She buried her face deeper in her arms, afraid of seeing that rejection in Nakor's eyes.

Nakor walked over to stand next to Galadrion's huddled form. He gently rested a hand on her quivering shoulder. A moment later, she looked up. Nakor took a moment to study the blood and sweat that covered her face. Kneeling down in front of Galadrion, he looked into her eyes. Galadrion flinched slightly, and looked away. After a few minutes, her trembling stopped. Resigned, she turned back to meet his eyes once again. There was no rejection in his eyes, only a mirroring of her pain. Nakor smiled slightly. It was a very soft smile, different from his usual, obnoxious grin. When he spoke, it was in a gentle, compassionate tone.

"Come home when you're ready."

> "And maybe, you know, brush your teeth first."

Having said that, he squeezed her shoulder gently, then turned and walked back through the forest. Galadrion began shaking again. Home...

Nakor walked into the ruins in which he had lived for the past year. There were only a few rooms left intact. The majority of the ancient castle was today little more than a mass of broken gray stone and shattered foundations. Shutting one of the few remaining doors behind him, he walked toward his makeshift dining room. Up ahead he could hear the high pitched voices of the two pixies.

Pynne was hovering in the air, studying a small owl who perched on a wooden stand. Its feathers were a deep red, almost black in color. The bird would occasionally flap its wings and make threatening noises at Pynne, who was floating nearby.

"His name is Flame," Nakor said. "His parents were killed by poachers while they were hunting."

> Even the bird has a tragic backstory.

He reached out to ruffle the feathers around Flame's neck. The bird twisted his head sideways and let out a quiet chirp of pleasure.

"He's beautiful," Pynne commented softly, studying the small owl. Flame was tiny for an owl, with a wingspan of just two feet.

At that point, Whoo flew into the room and landed in the center of a rectangular stone table. He was a curious being, even for a pixie. His first reaction upon entering Nakor's home had been to race from room to room, exploring and snooping.

Nakor grabbed a sack from a corner of the room and pulled out a loaf of bread he had bought earlier that day. It was placed on the table, followed by a block of cheese. Whoo, still standing in the middle of the table, promptly sat down and began to eat.

> If you've read Dianna Wynne Jones' wonderful *The Tough Guide to Fantasyland*, you'll know the only acceptable meals in Fantasyland are bread, cheese, and stew.

After retrieving some fruit from another sack, Nakor dipped a cup into a barrel of water and sat down at the table. Pynne flew to the table and tore off a piece of bread.

"So who were your little friends?" Whoo asked, taking a bite of cheese.

The grin on Nakor's face slipped for a moment. Images flashed through his mind. For the most part, they were images of death. The deaths of friends.

"That's a long story," he answered.

Whoo looked at him curiously. "You're our host, you

know. It's your job to keep us entertained."

Nakor looked him curiously.

"He's right," Pynne chimed in. "You have an obligation to your guests." She smiled sweetly and took a sip of water.

"Besides," Whoo added, "I'd like to know who I killed today."

Nakor set his cup on the table and sighed. "It's not terribly entertaining," he warned.

They just looked at him expectantly.

"About two years ago," he began, "I was met by an elf dressed in black robes. The same as the elf you saw today."

"He asked me to attend a 'meeting,' and paid me in gold before I even had the chance to consider it. I decided that it couldn't hurt, so I let him lead me to a small cabin in the woods."

> Nakor has obviously never watched a single horror movie in his life...

"Welcome," said the man in the doorway. Another elf, Nakor noted in his mind.

"My name is Calugar. Please come in."

Nakor's guide vanished back into the woods. With a shrug, Nakor stepped into a large, open room. There were five others who seemed to be waiting, sitting peacefully on the floor. All save one, a dwarven warrior who stood sullenly in a corner.

"Nakor, meet Roth, Serina, Brigit, Scrunchy, and Tetichitoani."

> Also known as the characters from my college D&D group. Because if there's one thing I've learned, it's that *everyone* wants to hear every last detail of your latest role-playing game!

Nakor nodded at each of them in turn.

"Roth and Brigit are wielders of magic, like yourself," Calugar continued. "The others prefer less mystical means of defense."

Nakor took a seat next to Brigit and Serina. Brigit was a plainly dressed woman with a long blond braid down the middle of her back. Serina was a bit more unusual. She was dressed in a leather breastplate and bracers, with a sword at her him.

> I assume that was supposed to be "…at her hip," but proofreading is for loosers!

"Five thousand years ago," Calugar began, "the god Kohut was imprisoned by his evil brother, Panich. Kohut was respected throughout the land as a just, fair god who blessed his followers with plentiful food and freedom from disease, among other gifts."

"Through the treachery of Panich, he was cast into an astral prison, where he had remained ever since. Kohut's follower's have dwindled through the years. Only a few of us still remain today."

> Another chapter has been infested with invasive apostrophes. I thought I sprayed for those.

"So what does this have to do with us?" Scrunchy piped up.

Nakor glanced over, noting the polished dwarven axe at his belt. Scrunchy, like most dwarves, had taken a nickname to use when he interacted with other races. Most dwarven names were unpronounceable to outsiders.

"After five thousand years of searching, we have discovered a way to free Kohut from his prison. Inside the nearby temple of Panich are six jewels. These are the very tools used by Panich to trap his brother. We have learned that they can also be used to free him."

> Am I the only one hearing that guy's name as "Panic" in my head?

"I need six people who are willing to retrieve those gems from the temple and participate in the spell to return Kohut to his rightful place among the gods."

"And why would we do this?" Brigit asked absently. She feigned disinterest quite well, Nakor thought.

"The jewels themselves are quite valuable, and would make a more than suitable reward I think. You are welcome to keep them, after the spell is performed. But more importantly, I ask that you do this to right a wrong that has lasted for hundreds of generations."

"How valuable are these jewels?" Scrunchy asked.

Calugar smiled. "Each one is approximately the size of a man's fist."

Scrunchy immediately made a fist and studied it. A grin spread across his bearded face. "When do we leave?"

Hours later, they walked toward a small crack in the cliffside.

> Wait, what cliffside? What just happened? I thought they were in a cabin in the woods. Where are they supposed to be now?
>
> "Shut up and stop asking so many questions."

"I am unable to enter the temple of Panich, except to cast the spell of freedom," Calugar called out from behind them. "But I shall be waiting for you when you return."

The six of them entered the temple, but only five emerged, days later. Scrunchy and Serina had gotten into an argument on the second day. They had been on the verge of coming to blows when Scrunchy turned and stormed away in a rage. It had been hours later when the rest of the party stumbled upon his remains. Nakor shivered. The rats who lived in the temple were thorough. It had not been a pretty sight.

> Poor Scrunchy. Healers continue to search for a
> cure for "Killed off because the player got bored
> and wanted to make a new character."

Calugar welcomed them back, healing their wounds. He had found a young girl to replace Scrunchy in the spell, a magician named Caudi. Later than night, he led them into the temple and began his spell, the spell he claimed would free his god, Kohut.

It was, for Nakor, one of the worst mistakes of his life. As the spell was cast, a searing pain ripped through his body. When it ended, Olara, a goddess of evil, stood before them all. "The Spider Goddess," as she preferred to be called. She looked at them all for a moment, then winced in pain. Seemingly unable to tolerate being within the temple that had imprisoned her for so long, she fled into the darkness of the night.

"You lied to us," Serina hissed angrily.

Calugar nodded. "I did," he admitted. "It was the only way to accomplish what was necessary to free Olara. I do apologize for deceiving you."

"You apologize?" Roth asked incredulously. In disgust, he sent a bolt of magic at the elven priest. Effortlessly, Calugar deflected the spell into the ground.

"If you do not leave now," he warned, "you will be destroyed. This is not my wish, but it is the will of my mistress."

Olara eventually killed him for allowing them to leave.

Over the next few months, the surviving members of the party were killed, one by one. Serina and Wanni were killed together, while hunting for food. Caudi had been assassinated as Nakor watched helplessly, too late to do anything but slay her assassins. Roth had been killed by a mounted knight who ran him through with his lance.

Less than a month after freeing Olara, Brigit and Nakor

had decided their only hope of survival lay in getting as far away from Olara as possible. Brigit had traveled hundreds of miles north, where she lived still. Nakor had gone in the opposite direction, making his home in an abandoned castle.

"That was two years ago," Nakor concluded. "Olara has left me alone ever since, until today."

"Are you sure that was one of her priests?" Galadrion asked.

He looked up. Galadrion was standing in a corner of the room, listening. He hadn't even heard her walk in.

"The one in the black robes was," Nakor answered. "The amulet around his neck was shaped like a spider. Olara's other title is 'The Spider Goddess.'"

"Why?" Whoo asked.

Nakor frowned. "I really don't know."

> Because it's SCARY!

Pynne glanced over at him. "These priests sound like nasty little footerlings," she commented, biting into an apple with a crunch.

Nakor grinned at the casualness of the remark. "Calugar had the decency to let us go free, and Olara killed him for that decency. Other than that, I've never heard of her followers being anything but evil." He cocked his head. "Footerlings?" he asked, raising an eyebrow.

> Raised eyebrow count: 4

"You ground bound people," Whoo explained.

He looked as if he was going to say more, but was interrupted by the sound of the castle's door being slammed open. "I'll go check that out," Galadrion offered, drawing her sword. Nakor looked her in the eyes for a moment, then nodded. Galadrion was a vampire, and that did give her the ability to protect herself better than anyone else at the table.

He eased his chair back from the table and stood up. Nakor rarely had visitors, and the timing of this intrusion made him uncomfortable. He trusted Galadrion to take care of herself, but he still wanted to be prepared. Glancing at the two pixies, Nakor loosened his rapier in its scabbard.

It was then that they heard the scream. A hoarse, inhuman scream, but it was definitely Galadrion's voice. Whoo and Pynne both vanished and flew toward the main hall. Nakor vaulted over the table and followed closely behind.

When they emerged into the hall, the first thing they saw was a large elf wearing the same black cloak as the priest they had encountered earlier. He held a small, silver amulet in the shape of a stylized spider in an outstretched hand.

Galadrion was huddled in the corner of the room farthest from the elf. There she clutched her knees to her chest, shaking violently. Her sword was lying uselessly on the floor.

> It's a little thing, but I wish I could walk through this manuscript with my Editorial Boots and stomp out the word "was" from bits like this. It's so much cleaner to write: "Galadrion huddled in the corner..." or "Her sword lay uselessly on the floor..."

Nakor drew his sword and was halfway to the intruder when the elf spoke.

"Tell your friends to stay back," the priest commanded in a menacing voice.

Nakor paused, confused. If he was asking about friends, that meant he could see the pixies. Nakor opened his mouth to shout a warning.

"Very well," the elf muttered. Before Nakor could act, the priest raised his other hand. A web of fire shot out from his fingers, coming to rest on a spot in midair. Nakor could see Whoo's writing form outlined against the flames. A moment later, the flames disappeared and Whoo fell to the ground. His wings had been burned away, and thick clouds of smoke rose from his hair and clothing.

"Pynne, stay back!" Nakor shouted.

"Right," Pynne said. "I'll just be over here, out of the way." She flew over to Whoo, examining the extent of his injuries.

The elf had tucked his amulet inside his cloak and was drawing a sword. Moving with incredible speed, he stepped forward and lashed out at Nakor.

Barely avoiding the strike, Nakor leapt back and drew his rapier. As he raised the weapon into a guard position, it was smashed out of his hand. He blinked in shock. Either this elf was the strongest Nakor had ever seen, or he wasn't playing fair. Nakor ducked under the next swing and slipped a dagger from his boot.

> Yes, I know Nakor had already drawn his sword just a few paragraphs earlier. But this was important, so I had him draw it twice.

Using the dagger to shove the elf's next thrust aside, Nakor danced backward, trying to put distance between them. His rapier was on the other side of the priest, out of reach. Frustrated, Nakor cast a quick spell.

The elf blinked in surprise as Nakor opened his mouth and let out a harsh shriek. Then he grinned as Flame came flying into the room, darting past him.

"You've got to be joking," he said with an evil smile.

Flame swooped down to grab Nakor's rapier in his talons. Straining his small wings, Flame lifted the sword and began to fly toward Nakor. With a laugh, the elf sent a web of fire that enveloped the bird.

Nakor smiled slightly as Flame flew, unharmed, to drop the rapier in his hand. After ordering Flame out of the room, Nakor turned back to the priest who had broken into his home. "It's called an 'Owl of the Forge,'" Nakor explained, raising his sword into a defensive position. "They make their nests in active volcanoes. I don't think you're little spell bothered him very much."

> A small companion animal with fire-related powers? Yes, it's true. Flame was the seed of an idea that eventually became Smudge the fire-spider in my Goblin and Libiomancer books.

The elf lunged forward, swinging his sword with a snarl. Nakor stepped to one side and neatly brought his dagger up to slice his arm. "Getting a little sloppy, are we?" he asked with a grin.

Then he was leaping backward, trying desperately to parry the furious attack the elf launched. Nakor had always had the bad habit of taunting his opponents. It looked like it might have gotten him into trouble this time.

Suddenly the elf spun around in a complete circle, swinging his sword to cut Nakor in half. Nakor leapt back, stumbling to the ground as he tried to avoid the blow. The elf's sword came speeding down, and Nakor brought his dagger and rapier together in an 'X' inches above his head. He winced as the elf's sword impacted with his weapons.

"Bad idea," Nakor said with an evil grin. Then he raised a booted foot and planted it squarely between the elf's legs.

> How do you know it's a Jim C. Hines book? Because sooner or later, someone's gonna get kicked in the crotch. Also, there will be fart jokes. But in my defense, kicking an elf in the crotch is pretty funny.

He was rewarded with a satisfying squeal from the elven priest. A moment later, the elf fell to the ground, clutching his injury.

Nakor sheathed his dagger and stood up. Reaching over, he plucked the sword from the hand of the moaning elf. Returning his rapier to its sheath, Nakor grabbed the priest by his cloak and slammed him into a nearby wall.

"I'll ask you once," Nakor said in a low voice, "Why are you here?"

The priest responded by pulling a dagger from his sleeve.

For once, Nakor was a second too slow. He managed to catch the priest's wrist, but then a fist slammed into his jaw. Nakor saw white for a moment, and then he felt the priest's knife plunge into his right shoulder. Pain shot through his body, and sweat broke out on his face. "Oops," he muttered, stumbling back.

Nakor drew his rapier with a wince. Taking it in his left hand, he readied himself for the next attack. Left handed, he knew that he was no match for this priest's fighting skills.

The priest took a moment to study Nakor. A crimson stain that was slowly spreading across his shirt, framing the dagger that protruded from his shoulder. Slowly raising one hand, the priest grinned.

"It was a nice try," he said, "but my mistress has ordered that you be destroyed." Saying this, he launched his web of fire at Nakor, smiling as the flames danced over his body.

Nakor closed his eyes. Of all the elements, fire was the one with which he was most skilled. As the flames touched his body, Nakor reached out with his mind. He could feel the magical energy being used to guide the flames.

With a mental nudge, he redirected that energy so it flowed around him. Nakor felt the scorching heat of the flames as they surrounded his body, and then they were gone.

> You might ask why Nakor has this convenient ability. Because MAGIC, that's why!

Stepping forward, Nakor stabbed the astonished priest

in the throat.

Remembering something a healer had once said to him, he left the dagger remain in his body for the moment, hoping that it would slow the bleeding. Wincing at the agony that shot through his right side, he wrenched his sword out of the body.

Kneeling down, he cut several strips from the priest's cloak. "Pynne," he called out weakly. As the pixie flew to him, Nakor studied the dead priest's hands.

Finding what he was searching for, he slipped a plain gold ring off of the priest's right index finger. He thought back, remembering the first time he had seen the ring.

> Even injured and possibly dying, Nakor is an experienced gamer and knows the importance of stopping to loot the body.

Calugar had worn it, using it to cast webs of flame on a band of goblins who had raided his home. "It is the ring of the high priest of Olara," he had explained. "It enhances the wearer's skills and strengths tenfold."

Pynne landed beside Nakor, and he slipped the ring into a pouch at his belt. "Whoo's alive," she said without pre-amble. "He's in pretty bad shape, though." Studying Nakor, she added "You look like you're rather messed up your-self."

Nakor managed a wry smile. "Forgot to duck," he commented. "I only have the strength to heal one of us right now, and I think that Whoo needs it most. But I'll need you to help me bandage this shoulder."

Pynne nodded. Nakor handed her a folded piece of cloth. Then he took a deep breath. He rested his left hand on the hilt of the dagger. Rolling his eyes heavenward, he jerked the knife from his body.

As Nakor gasped in pain, Pynne pressed the cloth onto the wound. Nakor took another breath, then held the cloth in place for her. He nodded at the strips of cloak, and Pynne used them to tie the makeshift bandage into place.

He waited a moment, hoping the pain would diminish. It didn't. Suppressing a groan, he reached out and used the wall to help him stand. Pynne hovered closely as he walked to where Whoo lay, still smoking slightly. Nakor sat down and laid a hand on Whoo's body. He muttered a few words, wincing with the effort. A moment later, the worst of the burns began to heal themselves.

Whoo looked up. Groaning, he asked "What did he hit me with?"

Pynne sat down next to him. "Fire. Lots of fire." she answered. Then she looked at Nakor questioningly. "When will you heal his wings?"

"I can't," he answered sadly. "There was nothing left to heal."

Whoo was in shock. He craned his neck, looking at the cauterized stubs protruding from his back. A pixie's wings were what made one a pixie. Many pixies who lost the ability to fly committed suicide, unable to withstand the grief. Those with the strength to survive lived life as a cripple, forced to walk in order to travel. The thought of living the rest of his life that way was unbearable. Whoo was still young, with many years ahead of him.

"I don't understand," he whispered.

"There's nothing more I can do here," Nakor said.

A thought struck him. "There is someone who might be able to help," he added. "I'll take you there once the rest of your burns have healed. For now, just try and sleep."

"Sleep?" Whoo demanded, outraged. Suddenly furious, he struggled to get to his feet.

Nakor concentrated, allowing what little energy he had left to flow into his voice. "Sleep," he repeated, resting a hand on Whoo's forehead.

> I think Nakor was a druid/thief, but as you can
> see, there's really no rhyme or reason to what he

| can or can't do. |

Whoo's protests gradually faded to a quiet mumbling, and his eyes drifted shut. A few moments later he began to snore. The corners of Nakor's mouth turned up slightly, a faint shadow of his usual grin.

"Stay with him, please," he said to Pynne.

The grin fled from Nakor's face as he turned to look at Galadrion, still curled up in a corner of the room. Holding his shoulder, he stood up and walked quietly to where she lay.

"Galadrion," he whispered, kneeling down beside her.

There was no response. She was still trembling, clutching her knees to her chest. Nakor looked at her hands. Galadrion's fists were clenched so tightly that blood dripped from within them where her fingernails had pierced the skin. Nakor had seen swords and arrows that were unable to break through that skin.

"Galadrion!" he repeated, more sharply this time.

She continued to stare blankly into space. Nakor took a deep breath. Drawing back his hand, he slapped her across the face with all of his strength.

| Nakor is not as knowledgeable about first aid as he likes to pretend. |

Galadrion blinked. Nakor grimaced and clutched his hand. When she still failed to respond, he swung again.

Instinctively, Galadrion caught Nakor's arm and threw him across the room. Nakor tucked his head and rolled. The blood drained from his face as pain shot through his body. Holding his shoulder with one hand, he crawled back over to Galadrion.

Seeing the she was looking at him, rather than through him, Nakor spoke again. "Galadrion?" he asked in a gentle voice.

"Nakor?" she replied softly. Tears began streaming

down her face. "What happened?" she asked.

Nakor thought back, remembering what had been going on when he walked in. Galadrion had been collapsed in a corner, and that priest was standing in the doorway, holding his amulet in one hand. Understanding came, sending an icy wave of fury through his heart. Some religions considered vampires to be unholy creatures of darkness. Priests of these orders had the god-given ability to use their faith to drive vampires away. Armed with a crucifix, amulet, or some other holy symbol, many such priests could completely destroy the undead.

He reached over and rested a hand on her shoulder. "He used magic on you," he said.

> "He made a successful roll to turn undead. Page 32 of the *Player's Handbook*."

Galadrion looked at him through her tears. "It had something to do with my being a vampire, didn't it? I could feel it."

Nakor nodded once. Anger mixed with self-loathing raced across Galadrion's face. She began to cry harder, burying her face in his shoulder.

> Remember, guys, it's fine to write powerful female characters, but only if they have to turn to a man for true strength and support!

After a while she stood suddenly, wiping the tears from her face. Without looking at anyone, she walked swiftly into another room. Nakor watched sadly as she went.

Pynne flew over to land next to him.

"How long will Whoo sleep?" she asked.

"Long enough for us to get him to help," Nakor answered.

Pynne nodded in understanding.

With a wry grin, Nakor looked down at the pixie.

"Wake me in a few hours, okay?"

Laying back onto the floor, Nakor immediately lost consciousness.

Pynne flew back to Whoo's sleeping form. Sitting next to him, she waited.

Nakor awoke with a start. The memory of the night's events raced through him, followed quickly by the pain in his shoulder.

"You awake now?" Pynne asked. She had been gently shaking his uninjured side for close to a minute.

"Yes," Nakor answered. Concentrating, he placed a hand on his wound. Frowning with the effort, he gradually healed the deep puncture made by the priest's dagger.

A few minutes later, he staggered to his feet. Tearing the bandage from his shoulder, he walked into the room Galadrion was in.

She was sitting in a corner, looking miserable.

"Are you okay?" Nakor asked, concerned.

Galadrion just looked at him.

"We need to leave here, soon," Nakor continued. "There's no way of knowing when Olara will send another attack."

> Maybe you should have thought of that before taking your elf-nap?

Slowly, Galadrion got to her feet. Walking as if in a daze, she followed Nakor out of the room.

Whoo still slept peacefully under Pynne's watchful eye. She glanced up as Nakor and Galadrion walked in.

"Let's go," Nakor said, lifting Whoo in his arms. Together, they walked out of the castle.

Silently, Nakor sat down on the grass and gestured at the others to do likewise. Once they had complied, he closed his eyes and began another spell.

His short nap had been too little time to completely replenish the magical energy he had expended earlier. Beads of sweat appeared on his face as he used his will to manipulate what little power he still had.

A short time later, he opened his eyes and let out a deep breath. Nakor gestured with one hand, using the other to hold Whoo in his lap.

Together, they began to rise, suspended on a carpet of air.

"If you can fly, why do you waste all your time on the ground?" Pynne asked.

Nakor allowed a smile to appear on his face for an instant. "It's a secret," he answered.

"Would it be easier if I flew on my own?" she offered impishly.

"It might," he responded, "but I don't think you'd be able to keep up with us."

Pynne looked at him with disbelief clearly etched on her face. "You'll have to prove it to me."

As they cleared the tops of the trees, a smile spread over Nakor's face.

"As you wish." He made a small motion with his index finger.

> That day, Pynne was amazed to discover that when Nakor was saying "As you wish," what he meant was, "I love you."

Pynne grabbed reflexively at Nakor's cloak as they shot forward. Her hair and clothes flapped madly in the wind as they flew at incredible speeds.

It was a bright night, well lit by the stars and the moon. She hated to admit it, but Nakor had been right. They were racing through the air faster than she had ever flown before. It was exhilarating.

Cautiously, she stood up. There was nothing beneath her feet, and yet it felt as if she was standing on something solid. The air on which she stood had a slight give to it, feeling slightly swamplike. With a smile, she spread her arms and let the gusty winds buffet her small body.

Nakor sat silently, lost in thought. Ever since he and Brigit had fled two years ago, Olara had seemed content to leave them in peace. Now, suddenly, there had been two attacks in the same night. What had changed, he wondered silently.

He slipped the priest's ring out of his pouch and studied it. That had been Calugar's ring, before he had been murdered by Olara. Apparently, his death was important enough that Olara had been willing to send her high priest out to kill him. It made no sense. Why now, after two years, would she suddenly be so intent on killing a lone elf?

> It's worth noting that at no point in this entire book does Nakor think to check on Brigit, or to send word that Olara is being all evil again. This reflects rather poorly on either him or the author. I leave it to the reader to decide which.

He dropped the ring back into his pouch. A better question would be, what was he going to do about it?

CHAPTER THREE

Nakor waved a hand, and they slowly began to glide downward. Soon, they came to a halt in front of a small, stone building in a circular clearing. Nakor stood up, mentally ending the spell.

> Some authors might have explained why Nakor can do magic, or what kind of powers he had, or what the limits were…anything to avoid the impression that he's simply pulling spells out of his pointed ears without rhyme or reason. But I prefer to preserve the mystery.

Pynne had vanished the instant she felt them sinking toward the ground. Nakor glanced over at Galadrion, who still seemed pale and weak. He was worried about her. The attack by Olara's high priest seemed to have taken a lot out of her.

Noticing his stare, Galadrion turned and began walking toward the building. Unable to do anything else, Nakor followed. Pynne flew invisibly behind them both.

It was an simple, stone structure. The doorway was a simple arch that framed a sturdy-looking oak door. In front of the door stood a large, burly man wearing white robes and holding a heavy wooden club. A plain copper amulet hung around his neck. To Nakor's eye, the amulet and the white robes marked him as an initiate of some sort.

He watched without speaking as Nakor and Galadrion approached.

"Our friend needs healing," Nakor said with a nod towards Whoo.

The initiate glanced at the unconscious pixie, then peered closely at Galadrion for a moment. "You may enter," he began, "but the undead are forbidden within the temple."

Galadrion turned away. An expression of pain raced across her face, but it was gone so quickly that anyone not watching would have missed it completely.

Nakor had been watching, and felt a wave of fury pass through him as he witnessed Galadrion's pain. He reached out and caught her arm as she began to walk away. Turning back to the initiate, he spoke in an even, quiet voice. "The undead is my friend, and she stays with me."

The white robed man simply adjusted his grip on the club and looked at Nakor in an appraising, calculating sort of way.

Forcing back his anger, Nakor asked in a tight voice "Then could you send a healer out to see us?"

The initiate shook his head silently.

Taking a deep breath, Nakor turned and gently passed Whoo's body to Galadrion. "We don't have time for this," he muttered.

Turning back around, Nakor cast a spell. He used his anger and frustration to supplement his minuscule reserves of energy. Even with that extra power, he swayed unsteadily as he finished his spell.

Stepping forward, the initiate raised his club to strike. Unfortunately for the initiate, the club now had different ideas.

Touched by Nakor's magic, the wooden club suddenly remembered what it was like to be alive and to grow. And grow it did. Branches shot out of the club and wrapped themselves around the initiate's arm. Soon his entire body was enveloped by the newly animated club.

Nakor stepped past the helpless guard and tried the door. It was locked. Ignoring the initiate's glare of defiance, he turned around.

"Galadrion?"

She handed Whoo's body back to Nakor, who stepped out of the way. With no expression on her face, Galadrion calmly ripped the door off of its hinges, lock and all.

Nakor smiled to himself and walked into the temple, followed closely by Galadrion. Pynne began to follow, but then a thought struck her and she took a moment to hover in front of the initiate. A quick push, and then she turned and flew after her companions.

A muffled cry, followed by a crash, signaled the toppling of the temple guard. Pynne giggled softly to herself as she waited for Galadrion to wedge the door back in the archway. Leaving the door propped slightly off-kilter in the doorway, Galadrion turned and followed Nakor inside.

Once inside the temple, they stopped. The only item worth noting was a white marble altar at the far side of the temple. A number of doors scattered almost randomly along three of the walls. From one of these doors, two men emerged wearing the gray robes of temple priests.

"Welcome back, Nakor," said one.

"Our friend needs healing," he replied bluntly.

The other priest stepped forward. Studying Whoo's wingless body, he asked "How did this happen?"

"He was burned," Nakor answered.

The first priest raised an eyebrow at Nakor's blunt

manner. After a second, he turned to his companion.

Raised eyebrow count: 5

"See to him, Sorin."

The priest addressed as Sorin gently took Whoo from Nakor, then turned wordlessly and walked through another door.

"Your friend will be cared for," the remaining priest said.

"Thank you, Thomas," Nakor responded wearily. As his fatigue caught up with him, he sank down to sit on the floor. With a slight smile, Thomas joined him.

Galadrion remained standing. Fatigue had no meaning for her, and she rarely allowed herself to relax. Slightly apart from the others, she allowed her mind to wander. The attack in Nakor's home had awoke the self-loathing she habitually ignored. Now, she simply waited, alone in her hatred. It would pass in time. It always did.

After a moment of studying the situation, Pynne allowed herself to become visible, and landed gracefully beside Nakor. Thomas raised an eyebrow, but said nothing.

Raised eyebrow count: 6

He turned to look closely at Galadrion. She simply returned his stare, her face expressionless.

Looking back at Nakor, he said "I trust your judgement in bringing these strangers to our temple, but I doubt Anthony would have been so open-minded. If I may ask..." he concluded with a glance toward the broken door.

With a slightly sheepish smile, Nakor answered "He's fine. Somewhat...immobile, but fine."

"Unless he bruised something on the way down," Pynne added.

Thomas sighed quietly to himself. He grasped a silver amulet from around his neck, similar to the copper one the initiate had worn. He closed his eyes briefly.

Moments later, a man wearing white robes emerged from one of the doors. "Yes, Brother Thomas?" he asked politely.

"Go and assist Anthony," Thomas directed. He waited until the white-robed man disappeared. Then he studied Nakor carefully, noting the weariness etched into his features. "Would you care to tell me?" he invited.

Nakor hesitated only for a moment. Starting with his encounter with Whoo and Pynne, he began to describe the two attacks made by the Spider Goddess's priests over the past day. Galadrion and Pynne added what few details Nakor forgot to mention.

A half hour later, Nakor ended his tale. Thomas nodded and slowly began to speak, almost to himself.

"I remember when Olara returned, two years ago. A goddess, gone for five thousand years, was suddenly among us once more."

> Ever notice how these things always involve nice, round numbers? Why don't we ever see an evil goddess who vanished for 3,142 years?

Nakor looked down, feeling guilty. He had never quite managed to forgive himself for his part in that resurrection.

"The gods do not decide lightly to destroy one of their own," Thomas continued. "Yet this was their decision in Olara's case. They battled for over a hundred years. Eventually, they were able to imprison her, powerless, in an astral prison of their own fashioning. The physical manifestation of that prison was the very temple from which you freed her. She had been left there, trapped in another plane, ever since. The gods made the decision to allow her to survive in exile. They were unwilling to expend the enormous amount of energy necessary to kill a god. A rather unfortunate error on their part," he added.

Thomas paused to contemplate his audience. Nakor sat quietly, wearing his old, frequently mended purple cloak.

Beside him sat Pynne, dressed in flowing silken clothes whose silver material seemed to be woven from the clouds themselves. She frowned slightly as she listened to Thomas. Behind them stood Galadrion, her face expressionless. Thomas spoke again. "But you must know why they decided to try and destroy Olara in the first place."

> Two chapters after introducing Pynne, I finally think to describe what she's wearing. Up to this point, I just kind of visualized her in cutoff blue jeans and a Black Sabbath T-shirt.

He took a deep breath. "One of the things we try to teach here is that everything has its place in the world. Good, evil, pain, joy, all of it serves some purpose. It is for this reason that evil can be considered an impossibility."

Galadrion raised an eyebrow at that.

> Raised eyebrow count: 7

"You seem confused," Thomas noted. "Allow me to explain."

He looked off into the distance, trying to organize his thoughts.

> We interrupt this book for an amateur philosophy lecture.

"Those people whom we describe as evil are, for the most part, unaware of the harm they cause. Evil is often a rather inaccurate label for ignorance. While that ignorance may cause great harm, it rarely contains the deliberate cruelty implied by the label of 'evil.'"

"Even so, there are those who delight in cruelty. Yet what event could ever occur from which no good would emerge? The most painful experiences of our lives are often the very same experiences that teach us the most."

"Galadrion," he said, turning to address her. "Even your curse is not evil in itself. Look at the good that has come of it."

> Sure, your husband was murdered and you've become a blood-drinking killer and sunlight will turn you into instant barbeque, but on the bright side, there's only 43,000 words left in the book!

Thomas gestured at Nakor. "You were able to use your gifts to rescue a friend today."

"Even death is not an evil, but rather a natural and necessary process. Quite simply, evil does not exist in a pure form. Thus, while Olara is considered to be evil by most, this is not sufficient reason for her banishment."

He paused to take a breath before continuing. "The world is constantly changing. Empires crumble, children are born, grow up, and die. All of it changes. Even for the gods, things change."

"Olara was unwilling to change. Her ways became inconsistent with the rest of the universe. By deliberately refusing to alter her ways, Olara gradually became an artifact from the past. She became an alien thing, whose mere presence could cause the decay and corruption of those around her."

> She's like that guy down the street whose house is still decorated in avocado green, and carpeted in deep shag.

"As a goddess, Olara possesses incredible power. One aspect of this power is that she exudes a powerful aura. It twists the life around her, until that life becomes warped, consistent with her own alien nature."

> Basically, her power gives her the power to exude a powerful aura of power. Also, power!!!"

"She was weak when she returned to our world. But as she grows in power, her influence will expand until it devours all life on our world."

"So why have the gods allowed her to remain for the past two years?" Pynne asked.

Thomas smiled in amusement. "Who are we to know what goes on in the minds of the gods? Perhaps they are unwilling to expend the energy necessary for another century-long war. Or perhaps they are no longer strong enough to battle a god of Olara's primitive might."

> "Who are we to know the minds of the gods?" asks the guy who just got done lecturing about the gods' motives.

Nakor looked startled.

"Gods also age, Nakor," Thomas explained. "Religions die out, gods lose their worshippers. Nothing is forever. It may be that the gods of today are no longer a match for the gods of the past."

"What I do know," he added, "is that Olara must not be allowed to continue her existence on this world. It is not a matter of good or evil, it is a matter of survival. If Olara remains, she will eventually destroy everything."

"Everything," he repeated, emphasizing the point.

Then he looked into Nakor's eyes. To Nakor, it felt as if those eyes were piercing into his soul. He felt an uncomfortable urge to squirm, but suppressed it.

"And you must be the one to destroy her."

Nakor blinked. "Perhaps I'm just a little slow, Thomas, but would you mind explaining how you came to that conclusion?"

"You have never been in the underground vault, have you?" Thomas asked. Without waiting for an answer, he rose to his feet. "Follow me," he said, walking past the altar to the door directly behind it.

Confused by this sudden change of subject, Nakor got to

his feet and followed after Thomas. Pynne floated gently after, and Galadrion walked behind her.

Thomas opened the door, revealing a narrow, winding staircase that descended into darkness. Taking a step down, he paused to reach into a small niche in the left wall. He withdrew a smooth wooden stick, as big around as a man's thumb, with a silver sphere on one end. As soon as it emerged from its hole, the sphere began to glow, emitting a strong blue light.

"One of our bright initiates designed this," said Thomas, leading the party down the stairs. "It's rather ingenious, actually. We still haven't figured out quite how it works." He stopped at the bottom of the staircase. "Ah, here we are."

They stood before another wooden door. Unlike the other doors in the temple, however, this one had no handle. Instead, a circular copper plate had been bolted to the center of the door at chest level. It was relatively undecorated, with a small, round depression in the middle. Thomas took his amulet and placed it into that depression.

With a click, the door swung open. "We don't allow most people to get down here," Thomas explained as they passed through the doorway.

They entered into a large room, much bigger than the temple above. Rows of shelves filled the room. On a few of the shelves, different amulets, wands, and other items were neatly arranged. Other shelves held endless numbers of books. Built into the walls were hundreds of small holes, each about the width of a man's fist.

Thomas led them through the maze of shelves. After a while, he stopped and handed his glowing light to Nakor. He studied the wall for a moment, counting silently to himself.

"Ah, here it is," he said at last. Leaning down, he withdrew a scroll out of one of the holes in the wall.

"It gets so hard to remember which scrolls are in which

hole," he commented. The one he held in his hand was yellowed with age. He slipped the ancient ribbon off with ease, for the scroll held naturally to its tightly coiled shape.

> Our priesthood doesn't believe in the Dewey Decimal System! Or labels.

"If you could assist me," Thomas asked, looking at Pynne.

He handed one end of the scroll to the pixie, and gingerly began to unwind it. Once it was fully unfurled, the scroll was over six feet long. Thomas gestured for Galadrion to hold the other end, and took the light from Nakor.

"This is the collected works of Ellana, a priestess of Olara," Thomas explained, skimming through the document.

"She described a great spell that would free Olara, and return her to her rightful glory."

Thomas brought the light close, finding what he was searching for.

"However, she also wrote that 'Olara's new life shall be the means of her true death. Only one who restores the goddess will have the power to destroy her, and he shall strike her down with that power.'"

Thomas continued. "That was a rough translation of the original Elvish, but Ellana specifically referred to a 'he,'" He looked at Nakor. "You are the only surviving male who participated in Olara's resurrection."

> Sexist prophecy is sexist.

Nobody spoke for a moment. Then Pynne asked "Is there any reason we should believe this prophecy?"

Thomas nodded. "There are other predictions concerning Olara's priesthood in the scroll, all of which have occurred. The passage I read is one of the few which has not yet been fulfilled."

> All of the predictions have come true, except for the ones that haven't. Sounds legit.

He pointed to a spot near the end of the scroll. "Here, Ellana describes her own death, which occurred shortly after she completed the scroll."

"We believed this to be the only copy of Ellana's work," Thomas continued. "However, if Olara has become aware of the prophecy, it could explain the recent attacks against you."

Pynne chose this point to let out an enormous yawn.

> I know exactly how she feels.

"My apologies," said Thomas with a smile. "I will show you to a room you may sleep in for as long as you need."

Handing the light back to Nakor, Thomas took the scroll from Galadrion and began to carefully roll it back into its original form. Once finished, he slipped the ribbon over one end and set the scroll back into its niche in the wall.

Turning, Thomas led them back out of the vault, pausing only once to take a small trinket from one of the shelves. Upon returning to the main level of the temple, Thomas pointed to one of the doors. "It's a small room, but it will allow you to rest."

As the trio turned to go, Thomas gestured to Galadrion. She looked back.

Thomas handed her the small, round coin he had taken from the vault. As she looked at him with a questioning gaze, he explained. "I am aware of some of the difficulties you face. That will allow you to travel unharmed in daylight." He gave her a small pouch with a long drawstring that could be word around the neck.

> Anyone else curious who the heck Thomas is, or why he's helping our heroes, or what made him decide to hand a super-powerful item to a strange vampire? It's been a long time, but I think the answer was, "Because that's what I wrote on the outline."

Galadrion studied the small, golden coin. There was a stylized picture of the sun on one side, with symbols from some foreign language on the other. She nodded her head once in thanks, and dropped the coin into the pouch. Slipping it over her neck, she turned to follow the others.

The first thing they saw after entering the small room was Whoo, sleeping contentedly on a small straw mat. Pynne flew to his side immediately, examining his newly regenerated wings. Nakor smiled for a moment, then went over to collapse onto another mat. Galadrion unbuckled her sword and carefully placed it on the ground before sitting down in front of the door. There she watched, back against the door, as Pynne and Nakor joined Whoo in his slumber.

Nakor stood on the edge of a cliff, looking out into the sandy wastelands beyond. The sky was a deep red color, and the wind blew small whirlwinds of sand around his feet.

He turned around, trying to figure out where he was. "Galadrion?" he called. "Pynne? Whoo?"

"They aren't here, Nakor," replied a deep feminine voice.

Instantly, Nakor's rapier was out and ready. He looked around, searching for the source of the voice.

"Where are you, Olara?"

There was a brief shimmering of light to his left, and the Spider Goddess appeared out of thin air. "Hello, my friend," she said warmly.

She glanced at the sword in Nakor's hand. "I see," she

said with mock surprise, "you seek to destroy me." Her face took on an expression of pain, as if she were deeply hurt by Nakor's malevolence.

Suddenly she was armed. In one hand, she held a black sword. A stylized spider formed the crossguard, and the blade seemed to radiate darkness from within. In her other hand she held a matching dagger. "Very well," she said, anger rising in her voice, "if this is the way it must be."

Nakor had seen Olara's weapons before. He backed up a step, seeking to put distance between them. The magical blades were enchanted to be razor sharp, as well as being unbreakable. The real power, however, lay in their ability to drain the blood from a body within seconds, leaving their victims dead before they could fall to the ground.

Suddenly Olara lunged forward and swung her sword. Nakor stepped back, raising his rapier to block. He watched in despair as Olara's black sword sliced cleanly through his blade, leaving him defenseless.

Nakor took another step back and stopped, suddenly realizing that the edge of the cliff was right behind him. There was nowhere else to run.

Olara smiled sadly. "I'm terribly sorry, my dear Nakor. But surely you must have known the futility of your quest." Her voice grew louder as she spoke. "The gods themselves could not destroy me! And now, you truly seek to accomplish that which the gods could not?"

Her sword vanished. Nakor watched as she slowly took the dagger in her right hand, holding the blade in a throwing position. "I wish it didn't have to be this way," she said, a cruel smile upon her face.

As she raised her hand to throw, Nakor turned and leapt from the cliff. Her deep, mocking laughter followed him down as he fell.

He landed on the floor of a damp, dimly lit hallway, flat on his back. He looked up in confusion, then rolled to one side to avoid the axe that was descending from above toward the middle of his head. As the axe thudded into the ground, inches from his ear, Nakor grabbed it by the handle and rolled backward, bringing his feet over his head to kick the axe-wielding goblin in the stomach.

Nakor leapt to his feet as the goblin stumbled back. As the goblin was wrenching his axe from the ground, Nakor pulled his rapier from its sheath. Now where had that come from, he wondered, studying the undamaged weapon in his hand.

Once armed, it was relatively easy for Nakor to dispatch the goblin. He looked around, trying to figure out where he was now. He was in a long, narrow hallway. There was a slight musty smell in the air. It all seemed vaguely familiar somehow, as did the goblin who had attacked him.

> Dang. Even in dreams, it sucks to be a goblin.

Nakor pulled his dark purple cloak around him, using it to help blend into the darkness. Still holding his sword in front of him, he began to walk noiselessly down the hallway.

Up ahead, the tunnel branched off in two directions. Nakor stopped a little ways before the fork, for he heard noises coming from one of the tunnels.

As he watched, a pair of skeletons walked into view, their bone feet clicking against the stone floor. Each of them held old, battered swords in one hand and equally decrepid shields in the other.

> I have absolutely no idea what the point of this sequence was. Or why I never bothered to spell-check my manuscript.

Nakor stepped back, hoping to avoid being seen. But some magical sense of the animated dead alerted them to his presence, and they turned toward him.

With a sigh, Nakor stepped into the center of the tunnel. Holding his sword in a guard position, he raised his left hand and cast a spell. He didn't know how susceptible the skeletons would be to fire, but hopefully the distraction would give him time to escape.

Pain shot through his entire arm, and the world blurred briefly. Nakor blinked, to see the two skeletons still advancing.

The lead skeleton swung its sword, knocking Nakor's rapier aside and slashing him across the ribs. Nakor winced in pain and backed away, glancing down at the cut in his side. It was not a fatal wound, but it was a painful one. A look of shock crossed Nakor's face as he realized what had happened. His spell had failed. Taking a few steps backward, Nakor turned and ran.

As he stumbled along, holding his side, Nakor cursed to himself. He knew, now, where he was. Somehow, he was once again in Olara's temple, the same temple which he had entered two years ago when he had first freed the goddess. Nakor remembered the first time he had tried to cast a spell inside the temple. He remembered his surprise as the spell failed, sending pain through his body. Something about the temple had prevented anyone from using magic. Calugar had explained it as an effect of the incredible magic used by the gods in this place. It distorted the lesser spells used by mortals.

> Aha! That's right, this was a flashback-in-a-dream. How original!

Whatever the explanation, it complicated matters immensely. Nakor stopped to listen. The skeletons had fallen behind, but he could still hear their footsteps in the distance as they followed.

Sheathing his rapier, Nakor pulled a leather sling from his belt. He reached into his pack and withdrew a pouch, from which he took a small lead ball. Dropping the ball into his sling, he replaced the pouch in his pack and he waited.

As the clicking footsteps of his foes drew closer, Nakor began to twirl his sling overhead, still holding his side with one hand. The moment the first skeleton came into view, Nakor launched his small sling bullet.

The lead ball streaked through the air and impacted with the skeleton's skull, sending splinters of bone in every direction. It collapsed to the ground in a pile of bone and metal.

The second skeleton dropped its shield and picked up the sword of its companion. Holding a weapon in each hand, it advanced toward Nakor.

Hastily tucking the sling back into his belt, Nakor turned to run. If he could repeat this trick, he might be able to get away.

Behind him, the skeleton stopped. Drawing back its arm, it hurled one of its two swords at Nakor's retreating form.

Nakor stumbled to the ground as the sword sliced across his legs. He tried to stand, but the cuts on the back of his legs prevented it. Taking a deep breath, he rolled over and drew his rapier. There he waited, trying to marshall enough strength together to defend himself.

All too soon, the skeleton was there, swinging its sword. Nakor brought his rapier up to block the blow, feeling the impact numb his arm. Again the skeleton struck, and again Nakor parried. He was sweating now, as the skeleton began to beat through his defense. Then he saw an opening.

The next time the skeleton struck, Nakor again caught it on his rapier. Suddenly, he dropped his sword and grabbed the skeleton by the wrist. As it struggled to free its arm, Nakor drew his dagger with his free hand and lunged forward, wincing at the pain in his side and legs.

He shoved the dagger into the skeleton's backbone. Using all of his remaining strength, he twisted, trying desperately to separate its vertebrae.

The instant he succeeded, the skeleton collapsed into a

pile, joining its companion on the floor.

Dazed and bleeding, Nakor crawled away. After a while, he collapsed to the ground. He frowned, feeling a slight breeze on his face. He looked to his left.

Weakly, he studied the wall of the tunnel. From the floor, he could see a slightly irregular projection on one of the stones. Having nothing to lose, he pulled himself over to the wall and pressed it.

A door slid open, revealing a small room. Thankfully, Nakor crawled inside and shoved the door back into place. It took all of his concentration to heal the wound in his side. Then he cut strips from his cloak to bandage his legs. The cuts were shallow there, and he could deal with them later. Then, mercifully, he lost consciousness.

Nakor opened his eyes. Disoriented, he wondered why he was laying on a straw mat, and how his legs had been healed. Then he looked over and saw Whoo, snoring peacefully, while Pynne slept a little ways beyond.

Everything came rushing back to him. Moving quietly, so as not to wake the pixies, he rolled over, expecting to see Galadrion sitting by the door. But she was gone.

> She's off to see if Jim Butcher has any openings in his books for an extra vampire.

Concerned, Nakor stood up, wincing at the soreness in his back and shoulders. Between sleeping on the hard, unfamiliar ground and having such an intensely realistic dream, his muscles were in knots. He took a moment to rub a shoulder, allowing the healing magic to flow into his aching muscles. Moments later, he slipped soundlessly out of the room, and into the temple.

Galadrion was nowhere to be seen. Nakor walked to the temple entrance, where the door was once again mounted on its hinges. Raising an eyebrow at that, he opened the door.

> Raised eyebrow count: 8

Nakor blinked as the sunlight momentarily blinded him. He was shocked to realize that it had been just last night that he was sitting in his tree, watching the sunset. It felt like ages ago.

The white-robed initiate who stood outside the door watched him expectantly. It was not the same man whom Nakor had trapped the night before.

"I'm looking for my friend," Nakor said.

The initiate nodded. "She went in that direction," he said, pointing.

Nakor thanked him, and walked off to find Galadrion.

He found her sitting on a rock, watching the sky. "Galadrion?" he asked curiously.

"I saw the sunrise, Nakor." she said quietly. Her voice was trembling. "It came up over there, between those hills." She pointed to a spot in the distance. "I haven't seen the sun in twenty six years."

Nakor studied her, noticing the tiny pouch she wore around her neck.

She grabbed the pouch in one hand. "Thomas gave me a way to see the sun rise." There were tears running down her face, and she still stared at the sky in wonder.

Finally, she turned to look at Nakor. He was smiling, enjoying the happiness that shone from her eyes. For as long as he had known her, Nakor had never seen Galadrion happy. It felt good to see, and for a brief time it distracted him from his own troubles.

For a moment, they both sat there, allowing the peacefulness of the moment to last as long as possible. Then Nakor frowned, as memories of his dream came rushing back into his consciousness.

"What is it?" Galadrion asked, noting his change in mood.

"Two years ago, I made a mistake," Nakor began. "I set loose a force that could eventually destroy my world. It seems only fitting that I be the one to correct that mistake."

"But I can't shake the feeling that I'm not strong enough to do what needs to be done. Olara is a goddess, one that even the other gods are unwilling to act against. Who am I to challenge that kind of power? I'm just another elf with a slight gift for magic."

Galadrion looked at him, concerned. Nakor habitually exuded an air of careless confidence. To see him without that mask was disconcerting, to say the least. She searched for words to comfort him, but found none. Finally, she settled for resting a hand on his shoulder, unconsciously imitating Nakor's gesture from the night before.

Nakor glanced at her, smiling slightly. Then he began to describe the dream that was disturbing him.

"Olara slashed my sword in half like it was nothing. I was completely helpless as she backed me off of the cliff." He paused, feeling the helplessness overwhelm him for a moment.

"Then I was back in the temple." He looked at Galadrion. "It was just as it was two years ago. Scrunchy and Serina had been arguing again. They always seemed to rub each other the wrong way. I don't even remember what they were fighting about this time."

"I decided to look around while everyone else dealt with their little disagreement." He smiled ruefully. "I fell through a trap door into some underground tunnels, and got attacked by some animated skeletons."

"Skeletons?" asked Galadrion.

> "Page 106 of the *Monster Manual.* Didn't you do the reading?"

"When a necromancer, or some other wielder of magic tries to raise the dead, the body must be healed first. Otherwise you end up with zombies or skeletons, or worse.

Someone probably put the skeletons in the temple deliberately, as some sort of guard. They have no wills of their own, so it's easy to control them."

He paused to make sure his explanation was clear.

"I almost died down there," Nakor admitted. "My magic was useless, and one of them slashed me in the side. The other one cut my legs. After that, it's a hazy memory of crawling away and waiting for the others to find me."

"Eventually, they discovered the open trap door and came down to find me."

He looked at Galadrion for a while. "Almost everyone who was with me in that temple is dead now." He closed his eyes, the pain of those deaths still strong within his heart. When he spoke again, it was in a quiet, hesitant voice.

"It scares me to think that could happen again."

They were both silent for a while. Then Galadrion spoke. "You were only asleep for a couple of hours. You should go and get some more rest."

Nakor nodded, once. Then he squeezed Galadrion's hand, which still rested on his shoulder, and stood up.

Fear and concern momentarily forgotten, Nakor snuck back into his small room in the temple. As he lay down, he felt the weariness begin to overcome him once more. Within minutes, he was asleep.

Galadrion watched sadly as he left. It felt good that Nakor had been able to trust her enough to admit being afraid. She herself had been unwilling to trust others for years, now. Nakor was the first who had begun to penetrate that shield of distrust, but even he was kept at a distance. It was the only way she knew to keep herself sane.

For the first time in what seemed like forever, Galadrion thought about her husband. Devin had been a good man, but he had been weak. She had long since forgiven him for inviting a vampire into their home. Like Nakor, Devin had been a man who loved nature. She remembered once when he had woken her up in the morning and taken her out to the lake to watch the sun rise.

Everything comes back to sunsets and sunrises!

Tears stung Galadrion's eyes, and she wiped them away without noticing. That morning with Devin had been less than a week before he was killed.

The emotions were threatening to overwhelm her, now. Years of pain and loneliness fought to reach the surface. Angrily, Galadrion forced them down again, refusing to acknowledge such feelings. Clearing her mind, she turned to stare once more at the sun.

After a while, her features softened again. Her memories buried once more, Galadrion allowed herself to relax somewhat.

Hours passed. Galadrion continued to sit outside, marvelling at her rediscovery of the day. Pynne and Whoo both slept soundly, their exhausted bodies recovering from the exertions of the night before. And Nakor dreamed again.

Dazed, exhausted, and bleeding, Nakor pulled himself into the small room, leaving the scattered bones of the skeleton behind him. Once inside, he used all of his energy to heal the wound on his side.

That's right, it's another dream-flashback!

Examining his legs, he found that they had both received shallow slashes, with the right leg barely even scratched. He used a dagger to cut bandages from his cloak, and tied them around his injured thighs. Once that had been accomplished, he allowed himself to rest.

Hours later, he heard a metallic clanking coming from the hallway. Nakor smiled, recognizing the sound of Scrunchy's armor banging against itself as he walked. Using the door to pull himself to his feet, he walked out to rejoin his companions.

They led him back to the trap door, berating him all the way for running off like that. Once they climbed out up through the hole in the ceiling, the scolding quickly stopped as they continued to search for the gems. But Nakor limped for the rest of his time in the temple.

His vision blurred, and a moment later he stood in a grassy clearing. He blinked his eyes to clear them, then unwillingly took a step back.

In front of him lay Scrunchy's body, just the way they had found it. The rats had left little more than a skeleton, still wearing a silver breastplate and helmet, sword clutched in one outstretched hand. A pair of daggers lay on the ground by his waist. A brown rat peered up at Nakor from within the rib cage. After a moment, it scurried away and vanished.

> Suddenly, the book takes an unexpected turn toward the gruesome.

Nakor turned away, only to see two small stones set on a sandy beach. The fingers of his hands clenched, unnoticed, into fists. Nakor had not been there when Serina and Wanni were killed. They had been out hunting, less than a day after they had freed Olara. It was almost a week before Nakor, Roth, Caudi, or Brigit learned what had happened. Roth had heard a rumor of two strangers who had been found dead by the shore of the lake. According to the people who had buried them, Serina and Wanni were both pierced through the heart by a single arrow. They would have died instantly.

> "The fingers of his hands." As opposed to the fingers of what, his left armpit? What kind of weird anatomy do these elves have, anyway?

There was a snorting noise behind him. Knowing what was about to happen, Nakor tried not to look.

The dream took over, and Nakor felt himself turning to watch as a mounted warrior thrust his spear through Roth's unarmored chest.

> The snorting noise had nothing to do with any of this. Apparently, that was just a random pig wandering through the dream. Nakor's subconscious is a weird place.

Just as had happened in reality, Nakor felt pain and fury overwhelming him. He stretched out one hand, fingers spread, to point at the murderer before him.

The man turned his horse to look at Nakor.

> Wait, is the man looking at Nakor, or is he just trying to get his horse to look?

Drawing upon the power of the air itself, Nakor sent a blast of wind at the man that knocked him from the horse.

As he struggled to rise, Nakor raised his other hand. He used the pain and anger at the death of his friend to fuel his magic, drawing upon power he had never before allowed himself to use. Now, he used it with an almost insane rage, sending the man hurling through the air to smash against a large oak tree, back broken by the impact, just as had happened two years ago.

> "Use your aggressive feelings, boy. Let the hate flow through you. Strike me down with all of your hatred and your journey towards the dark side will be complete!"

Nakor sank to his knees, overwhelmed. Then he raised his head, knowing what must come next. As he watched, the young wizard Caudi raced into view, pursued by two men.

She turned and started to cast a spell, but one of the men hurled a dagger that lodged in her stomach. She stumbled backward.

Sprinting, Nakor tried to reach her in time, as he had been unable to in life. He was still too far away when one of the men stepped up and stabbed Caudi through the heart, killing her instantly.

Nakor slowed to a walk, watching as her body crumpled to the ground. One of the men yelled as he spotted Nakor approaching. The other looked up, and said "That's the other one we want."

They approached, swords drawn. Too numb to even attempt a spell, Nakor silently drew his rapier in one hand, dagger in the other, and waited motionlessly.

As the men neared, Nakor suddenly leapt into motion. He batted a sword out of the way, and almost casually stabbed one of the men with his dagger. Smoothly, he stepped back, avoiding a thrust by the other man's sword.

Seeing his companion bleeding out his life on the ground seemed to put fear into Nakor's remaining opponent. Gathering his courage, the man lunged again.

Nakor caught the sword on the long blade of his dagger, diverting the attack to one side. Then he smashed the basket hilt of his rapier into the man's face.

He stumbled backward with a yell, dropping his sword and clutching his hands to his face. Nakor brought the point of his rapier up until it touched the man's throat. Walking slowly, he backed the bleeding man up against a tree.

The rage was clearly audible in Nakor's voice as he spoke. "Who sent you?" he asked simply.

The man's voice was almost a whimper. "Olara."

Nakor killed the man quickly and cleanly. It was a far nicer death than he would have had otherwise, when Olara learned of his failure. Olara was not known for her tolerance.

He turned around, and discovered that he faced the entrance to Olara's temple. From within, he could hear Olara's mocking laughter echoing through the tunnels. Then she began calling out his name. "Nakor..."

"Nakor!"

Nakor jumped and opened his eyes. Galadrion was staring down at him, while Pynne and Whoo hovered nearby, looking concerned.

"I'm okay," he muttered. He sat up, still feeling tired. "How long have I been asleep?"

"It's midday," Whoo answered. "The rest of us have eaten already, but Thomas said not to wake you."

"But then you were having some sort of nightmare," Pynne added, "So we woke you up anyway."

Nakor smiled weakly at her logic.

"Nakor," Whoo said, "I have a question for you." He paused for a moment. "Where are we?"

"In a temple," Nakor replied.

Whoo rolled his eyes at that. "What kind of temple is this, and who are the priests who live here?" he demanded.

> Questions that would have made much more sense for someone to ask several scenes ago.

Nakor leaned his back against a wall and ran his fingers through his hair. "I don't know, exactly." he began. "I came to this area a year and a half ago, trying to escape from the death that seemed to follow me and those I cared about." He shivered once, recalling his dream.

"I had been following the river, and eventually it led me to the ruins of an ancient castle. While I was exploring it, I stumbled upon the family of bears that was already living there."

Nakor remembered his shock as he and the bear stared at each other, both uncertain how to react for a moment.

That moment had allowed Nakor to cast a spell, after which he spoke to the bear and assured it that he meant no harm.

"I lived with the bears for about a year," he continued, oblivious to the looks of surprise on his audience. "Then they took off to find someplace new." He smiled, remembering. "Apparently I made their cave smell like elf."

"A few days after I arrived, Thomas came to visit me. He invited me back here, to his temple. He never did explain exactly what god is worshipped here. From what I've gathered over the past year and a half, the priests are devoted to peace and knowledge. Aside from that, I know little of their religion. Once we arrived, he took me into a room and we sat down together. Then he began to talk to me. Talking about Olara..."

> You know how they say if your only tool is a hammer, then everything looks like a nail? I'm starting to think the only tool in my writer's tool box was the flashback.

Thomas had stared at Nakor for a long time, and neither spoke. Finally, Thomas broke the silence.

"It wasn't your fault," he said softly.

Nakor stared, confused, at this odd man in his grey robes. "I don't know what you're talking about." he replied.

"Calugar lied to you, he used you to free his goddess." Thomas explained. "There was no way you could have known."

Feeling suddenly vulnerable, Nakor stood up and took a step toward the door.

"Sit down, Nakor," came the soft voice of the priest. "You're safe here. I know about these things because they affect all of us. I could feel it when Olara was brought back. I spent the next few days trying to figure out how it was done, and who was involved."

He looked sympathetically at Nakor. "I also know what

happened to the others."

Nakor sat down hard. He rested his head in his hands and closed his eyes. "I should have been there. I was too slow to save Roth. Too late to save Caudi."

He looked into Thomas's eyes. "I wasn't even around when Wanni and Serina were murdered!"

"There was no way you could have been everywhere at once." Thomas answered in a gentle voice. "There was no way you could have known."

Nakor lowered his eyes again. When he spoke, his voice was pure bitterness. "I should have."

"And why is that?" Thomas asked. "Why were the lives of these people your responsibility?"

"What do you mean?"

Thomas looked at him sadly. "Each of your friends was just as responsible as you were for freeing Olara. Why do you take all of this responsibility upon yourself? No man can hold that much weight upon his shoulders."

A tear fell from Nakor's left eye. He clenched his fists and looked up at Thomas. "Who are you?" he demanded.

| "Stop intruding on my angsty elf-pain!" |

"Does that matter?" Thomas replied.

Something snapped inside Nakor. The months of pain and anger came rushing to the surface, and he stood up to grab Thomas by the front of his robe. "Of course it matters," he shouted.

Thomas grabbed one of his wrists, and the next thing Nakor knew, he was lying on his back, staring up at the plain stone ceiling. For a brief moment, he lay there, stunned. He blinked, and the emotions came rushing back. Rationality completely forgotten, Nakor stood up and drew his sword, levelling the blade at his foe.

| In Fantasyland, all monks are martial artists. |

> Which makes you wonder why Nakor didn't
> know what he was getting into…

Thomas watched, calmly, without reacting.

Gradually, the tip of the sword began to quiver. Then it was slowly lowered to the ground. There was a metallic crash as the rapier slipped from Nakor's hand. Overcome by despair, he sank to the ground and clutched his head in his hands.

> "My elf-pain is the ANGSTIEST elf-pain!"

Thomas walked over and lay a hand on his shoulder. Nakor looked up, tears flowing freely down his cheeks.

"You can sleep here tonight, if you wish," Thomas offered.

Nakor nodded, too overwhelmed to speak.

"I stayed for about a week," Nakor said, looking up at Galadrion, Whoo, and Pynne. "During the day, I did what work I could to help out. At night, Thomas and I would talk, sometimes for hours at a time."

Nakor smiled. "Since then, I've come here when I needed a place to rest, away from the rest of the world."

"So," began Whoo, "would any of these people have some idea as to how we're going to kill Olara?"

"We?" asked Nakor, raising an eyebrow.

> Raised eyebrow count: 9

"She burnt my wings!" Whoo replied, outraged. "I'm not just going to sit around and let her get away with that!"

Nakor looked over at Pynne.

"Every time I let him go off on his own, he gets in trouble." she commented, smiling evilly. "So I guess I should go to."

> Or go "too," even.

He turned to Galadrion, who simply nodded.

Taking a deep breath, Nakor addressed them all. "I don't know," he pronounced. "I don't know how to kill a goddess, and I don't know how to keep her from killing us if we try."

Silence fell over the room, as each person felt Nakor's despair spread out to touch them.

> "This is my elf-pain, which I share with you in the ancient elven ritual of the misery-meld. 'My angst to your angst. My pain to your pain…'"

At that point, there was a knocking on the door. Galadrion walked over to let Thomas into the small room.

"You must leave, soon." he said, sitting down to join them. "While you remain in our temple, you are safe from Olara's evil. But soon she will know where you have escaped to. Once that happens, it will be impossible to leave here without being killed."

Nakor stood up immediately, only to have Thomas laugh and motion for him to return to the floor.

"I said soon, Nakor," Thomas explained. "Not now. Before you leave, there are things you all must know."

> "I haven't finished infodumping yet!"

"Such as?" Pynne asked.

"When Olara first returned to this world, she was weak." Thomas began. "She was also vulnerable. For five thousand years, all of her power had been spent in surviving. It has been theorized that she would have eventually died there, once her power was completely depleted."

"Since the day of her rebirth, however, she has been steadily growing. Each day she gains in strength. Even after two years, she is not as powerful as she once was, though." He looked at Nakor. "This is why you still live."

Nakor looked confused.

"Have you never stopped to wonder why Olara didn't simply kill you herself?" asked Thomas.

Nakor nodded in response.

"Do you remember the pain you felt when she returned?"

"It was like something ripping me apart from the inside," Nakor answered.

"Not a bad description of what happened," Thomas said. "Each of you who participated in that spell felt the same pain. Almost as if part of your very soul was being torn from your body. In essence, that's exactly what happened. Olara took the very life from you all in order to survive. She needed that energy to recover from the shock of being thrown back into our world."

> For the record, I wrote this long before Harry Potter came out.

Thomas looked at Nakor. "That is what saved your life." He paused, trying to explain. "It's almost as if, by taking your life force, Olara became a part of you, and you of her. It leaves her unable to harm you without likewise harming herself."

"In other words," Whoo jumped in, "she can't kill Nakor without killing herself at the same time?"

> "Either must die at the hand of the other for neither can live while the other survives." —Sybill Trelawney, from the Harry Potter books. Which is exactly what I was trying to say, only J. K. Rowling did it much, much better.

"That's correct," Thomas said. "It isn't an exact explanation, of course. She was still able to send others to kill Nakor without the fear of harming herself. But more important is the fact that once she gains enough power, she will be able to rid herself of her tie to you."

"Once that happens, Olara will kill you."

> I think I gave that last line its own paragraph be-
> cause I thought it would add emphasis and
> drama. Instead of adding confused readers say-
> ing, "Wait, who the heck is talking now?"

"So how long do we have?" asked Whoo.

"I don't know." Thomas answered. "It has been two years. I suspect that Olara will have enough power soon, if she does not have it already. And once that happens..."

He let that sentence hang, unfinished.

"So what's to keep her from killing us the moment we leave here?" demanded Pynne.

"The coin I gave to Galadrion will hide you from her," came the response. "Provided you stay within fifty paces of it."

"Thank you," Nakor said.

"So how do we kill her?" Whoo asked, hovering in mid-air.

> Questing is hard. Fortunately, Thomas is here to
> spoon-feed them the answers. We're a step away
> from him giving them an instruction sheet by
> Ikea, with cartoonish diagrams and a little god-
> dess-slaying allen wrench.

Thomas sighed. "As far as I know, Olara's only weakness is her inability to re-enter the temple from which she was freed. Yet even that would not destroy her. It would just cause her intense pain."

"Intense pain is a good place to start," Galadrion said dryly.

"Perhaps," Thomas said with a slight smile, "but it is not enough. Which is why I need to tell you of Averlon."

He sat back against a wall. "Averlon was an elf, a member of our order who lived about two thousand years ago.

He was a minor priest, who for many years lived a simple and uneventful life."

"He worked as a scribe, copying and recopying various works in the vaults. But one day, he read something that frightened him. Terrified, he took the book he had been copying and threw it into a nearby fireplace, destroying it. By doing so, Averlon violated one of our most ancient laws."

I have strong feelings about book burning.

"Averlon's membership in our order was revoked, though he was invited to remain and live among us. But Averlon chose to leave, still terrified by what he had read. When asked about it, his only reply was to mumble about 'the spider.'"

Thomas paused to let the significance sink in. "Years later, Averlon returned. He was old, and dying. He had with him the dagger of Olara, the same knife Olara wears at her side today."

"He was ushered into the temple. There, we attended to his illness as best we could, but to no avail. It was a strange sickness, almost magical in nature. I suspect Averlon died an unnatural death. Oddly, though, he seemed content. The terror that had driven him away years before was gone."

"The night before he died, he talked of many things. His journeys, the dangers he had faced, the mistakes he had made. But he took great pains to insure we knew of a scroll upon which he had written a spell. He described it only as 'Olatha-shyre,' which means 'Spider's Bane' in an ancient elvish dialect. Unfortunately, all he revealed of the scroll's location was that it was 'safe from *her.*'"

Thomas looked at Nakor. "We have never been able to locate the scroll. We don't even know if it truly exists. If it is found, there is no way to say what the spell does."

"What happened to the dagger he brought with him?" asked Galadrion.

Thomas gazed somberly at her. "It vanished from our vault two years ago."

He frowned for a moment. "You must leave now." He stood up and escorted them to the temple's doors as he talked. "Olara's priests are approaching from the north. If you head south, then turn east, you should be able to make it back to your home without incident."

"Also, I'm tired of infodumping."

As they headed out the door, Thomas called after them. "Be cautious! I doubt Olara would be so considerate as to leave your home unguarded."

Nakor turned to express his thanks, but the door had already been shut behind them. Grimly, the four of them headed eastward at a swift pace into the forest.

CHAPTER FOUR

THEY WERE SEVERAL HUNDRED YARDS INTO THE woods when they heard the horses. Pynne and Whoo disappeared, and Nakor and Galadrion fell to the ground to hide among the ferns and bushes. Looking back, they watched as a group of men approached the temple.

A black robed priest was talking to the initiate at the door, while twenty men on horseback waited behind him. They looked like mercenaries, to judge from the assortment of weapons and armor displayed.

Even Nakor's elvish ears were unable to discern what was being said from that distance.

> "We're selling Spider Scout cookies to raise money for Murder Camp. Would you like a box of evil thin mints?"

The priest was saying something to the initiate. The initiate nodded, then turned and walked into the temple. A minute passed. Two. Five. The mercenaries began to fidget restlessly.

After ten minutes had gone by, the priest backed away and pointed at the door. Two of the largest men jumped from their horses and drew out large, heavy axes. As one, they began to hack at the door.

It soon became clear that their efforts were having no effect. The door stood without a scratch, despite their best efforts.

Gesturing for them to move out of the way, the priest stepped in front of the door. He pointed a hand, and a blue beam of energy shot out, only to dissipate in a shower of sparks, inches in front of the door.

He raised both hands, pouring more energy into his spell. Still, nothing happened.

Nakor tapped Galadrion on the shoulder.

"They could be there all day," he whispered with a grin. "Let's get out of here before someone intelligent shows up."

> Given what we've read so far, I don't think Nakor has anything to worry about.

Moving cautiously, they began to make their way through the forest.

Hours later, as the light was beginning to fade, they stopped.

"This was a much shorter trip when I was asleep," Whoo grumbled.

"If you'd like, I'm sure one of us would be willing to knock you unconscious again," Pynne shot back.

Ignoring both of them, Nakor sat down with a sigh. "I'm hungry," he announced to no one in particular. Then he began to pluck small red berries from a bush and pop them into his mouth. They were slightly sour, but Nakor didn't mind.

> Dear kids: don't eat strange berries in the woods.

The pixies flew over to join him, still arguing.

"If you would have kept up with me, maybe we could have killed him before he shot me!" Whoo said.

"If you had ducked, maybe you wouldn't have lost your wings to begin with!"

Rolling her eyes, Galadrion walked away and began to sharpen her sword. "If you had both stopped arguing, maybe the vampire wouldn't have ripped the tongues out of your heads," she muttered.

> Heh. Half my career has probably been based on writing snarky dialogue for various characters.

The conversation was interrupted as Nakor abruptly stood up and gestured for silence. Drawing his rapier, he stared out into the woods.

Moments later, a small girl came crashing through the undergrowth. She was human, probably about twelve or thirteen, Nakor guessed. The girl was barefoot, and dressed in tattered rags held in place by a rope belt. Her brown hair hung in ratty tangles around her face. She ran to Nakor, throwing her arms around his waist.

"Please don't let them hurt me," she cried frantically.

Nakor, feeling slightly foolish, patted her absently on the back while looking for a place to put his rapier. Not finding one, he tossed it to one side.

> If only someone would invent some sort of sword-holding device, perhaps one that could be worn on a belt.

"It's okay, you're safe." Perplexed, he looked at Galadrion, who shrugged.

"What's your name? Who are you running from?" Nakor asked.

"Jenn," she answered, sniffling.

"I'm Nakor. What's the matter? Who is it you're afraid

72 JIM C. HINES

of?"

She didn't answer, but continued to bury her face in his side.

"I'll go make sure there's nobody following," Galadrion offered.

Jenn jumped, startled. Spinning around, she looked at Galadrion. "Oh! I didn't see you," she said, embarrassed. Then she ran to Galadrion to embrace her as well.

> Because this isn't suspicious or creepy at all.

It was Whoo, floating invisibly to one side, that saw it. He was the only one at the proper angle to notice Jenn slipping a small pouch inside her shirt as she turned away from Nakor. He flew over to hover by Galadrion's shoulder.

Whispering quietly, so that only she could hear, he said "She's a thief."

> WHAT A SHOCKING TWIST THAT NONE OF US SAW COMING!

Galadrion's sympathy fled. Grabbing Jenn's rope belt with one hand, she lifted the small thief into the air. There she dangled helplessly, looking like a kitten being held aloft by its mother.

"Did I miss something?" Nakor asked, confused.

Instead of answering, Galadrion lifted Jenn higher until they were eye to eye. "Give it back," she said in a low voice.

Jenn squirmed, trying to escape. Seeing the futility of that approach, she turned to look at Nakor.

"Help me! I didn't do anything!" she pleaded. "Give what back? I don't understand." Tears were starting to fall from her eyes as she looked fearfully from Nakor to Galadrion.

"She's got a pouch she stole from Nakor tucked inside her shirt," Whoo prompted, still whispering.

"The pouch you stole," Galadrion said, "the one inside

your shirt. Give it back."

The tears stopped, and the look on her face changed to one of anger. "Fine," Jenn snarled. "Probably wasn't much in there anyway."

She reached up a sleeve and produced a dagger. Twisting around in Galadrion's grasp, she slammed the dagger into the arm that held her, helpless, in the air.

The blade tore through Galadrion's shirt, then skidded harmlessly across her skin. With her other hand, Galadrion slapped the knife out of Jenn's hand. Jenn cried out and grabbed her hand.

> How many times can you repeat the word "hand" before it starts to lose its meaning? Hand, hand, hand, hand, hand...

Pynne ducked as the knife went spinning over her head. "Watch it," she complained.

"You bitch, you broke my hand!" Jenn shouted. Suddenly she realized that the last voice she had heard came from empty air.

> "Bitch." When the author is just too darn lazy/sexist to come up with a more interesting insult.

Jenn got nervous. Always in the past, she had been able to talk her way out of trouble. Failing that, there was always her dagger. But now, with this witch who seemed invulnerable to weapons, and voices coming from nowhere, Jenn was afraid.

Rolling her eyes, Galadrion turned Jenn upside down, holding her by the legs. She gave one bone-rattling shake, and Nakor's pouch fell to the ground, followed by a flat leather package.

> I'm curious what was in that leather package, but

I'm pretty sure I forgot all about it by the next scene.

Pynne smiled. Still invisible, she carried the pouch back to Nakor and dropped it in his waiting hand.

Jenn's eyes widened. Then, she looked up at Galadrion. "So now what are you going to do with me?" she asked. The outrage in her voice managed to cover up the fear she was feeling.

"Oh, just let her go," Nakor muttered, retrieving his rapier from the ground.

"She's seen us," Galadrion replied quietly.

Nakor froze. The coin Thomas had given them would protect the group from magical detection. But if Jenn were to tell the wrong person what she had seen, Olara could track them down with ease. Yet what other options did they have?

"Hey, I didn't see nothing!" Jenn insisted nervously. "Just let me go, I won't tell anyone. I promise!"

"Let her go," Nakor repeated.

Wordlessly, Galadrion set her on the ground. The first thing she did was grab the leather package from the ground and replace it inside her shirt. Once that was done, Jenn backed away warily. After scooping her dagger from the dirt, she turned and ran.

"You believed her?" Galadrion asked.

"Nope," answered Nakor with a grin.

Whoo and Pynne both became visible at the same time. "So now what?" demanded Whoo.

Nakor just smiled. As he explained his plan, Galadrion fingered the torn sleeve of her shirt. "Stupid kid," she muttered to herself.

Jaimus and Erik waited impatiently in silence. Jaimus, the larger of the pair, sat cleaning his fingernails with a small dagger. Erik simply waited, eyes closed, as he leaned against a tree.

"She's late getting back," Jaimus complained.

"She's been slowing down for a while now," Erik commented. "She's getting to old to play cute and innocent anymore."

"So why don't we just find someone else?"

"Because it takes too long to break in a new kid," explained Erik. "Don't you remember when we first had to teach her all this stuff, back in the beginning?"

"Yeah," Jaimus muttered. "I'm gettin' tired of the brat, though. Last time, she tried to hold out on us. I had to knock her around real good before she'd give us the rest of the money."

Erik, who habitually kept more than his share of the money from both Jenn and Jaimus, rolled his eyes. "I was there, Jaimus. I remember."

"Yeah, well I'm just getting tired of her. That's all." Jaimus went back to cleaning his nails, occasionally stopping to wipe the tip of the knife on his trousers.

> "We are bad guys!" In case that was too subtle.

Hearing Jenn's approach, they both stood up. Jaimus slipped the dagger back into his boot.

Panting, Jenn stopped in front of the two men. There she took a moment to catch her breath.

The trio had been working together for years. Jenn had grown up in a city, the daughter of one of the most successful husband and wife teams in the history of the thieves guild. When she was still young, they had been set up by a fellow thief and murdered. Ever since, Jenn had survived on her own.

Erik had been a friend of her father. He had taken the girl in and taught her the skills she needed to be a thief. She had turned out to have a great deal of innate talent, pleasing both of them. With Erik's help, she had eventually managed to have the man who had murdered her parents killed.

Jenn's relationship with Erik had never been close, but it had been profitable. As long as she did what she was told, she got to keep a share of the money they stole. If she made a mistake, she was beaten. Jenn made few mistakes.

Lately, Jaimus had been working with them. The three of them had devised a plan that had kept them in gold for several months. Jenn would run up to unsuspecting travellers in the woods and steal what she could. She would then run back to Jaimus and Erik with an appraisal of the situation. If the travellers looked wealthy enough, Jaimus and Erik would attack, using surprise to kill and rob the unfortunate victims. They were both large men, skilled with their weapons of choice. Jaimus habitually carried a large, double-bladed axe, while Erik settled for a simple broadsword.

Jenn was an excellent thief. It was the only way to avoid the beatings that were the reward for failure. Now, having returned empty handed, she steeled herself for the punishment to come.

"Well?" Erik asked.

Unable to think of a believable excuse, Jenn settled for truth. "I didn't get anything. They caught me."

Erik raised an eyebrow. "They caught you. How odd." He shook his head. "The last time anyone caught you was two years ago, and even then you came away with their gold. So this pair must have been truly extraordinary, hm?"

Raised eyebrow count: 10

"I had it!" Jenn protested. "I had his money, but then the witch caught me! She had invisible spirits helping her. I tried to get away, but my knife just bounced off her arm!"

Erik listened patiently. "I suppose that's possible," he conceded. "But just in case, I think Jaimus should have a chat with you."

Jaimus smiled. "You wouldn't be trying to hold out on us, would you?" he asked, advancing.

Resigned, Jenn closed her eyes and waited. A moment

later, a loud slap rang through the woods, and Jenn fell.

> Writing tip: villains don't all have to be over-the-top, child-beating, puppy-kicking, moustache-twirling, black-hat-wearing caricatures of EVIL. This whole scene is making me cringe more than anything else in the book so far.

She moved her jaw, making sure it wasn't broken. As she struggled to rise, Jaimus hit her again.

> Because he's EVIL.

Erik walked over and knelt in front of her. Shaking his head, he said "I'm sorry Jenn, I truly am. But, well, I'm afraid that I don't believe you."

Jenn spat blood out of her mouth. "So search me," she demanded.

"Oh no, little one," he replied sadly. "I know you're much too clever for us. You probably hid the gold in the woods, hoping to come back for it later." He grinned. "It's what I would have done."

Erik stood back up. "It just seems like we can't trust you anymore. It's too bad, really. You had a lot of talent."

He nodded to Jaimus. "I guess you were right. Maybe it is time for a new partner."

Jenn drew her dagger and lunged at Jaimus. Moving swiftly for his size, he reached down and caught her by the wrist. Squeezing, he forced the dagger from her hand, then used his other hand to send her crashing into a tree.

Dazed, Jenn slipped to the ground again. Erik was drawing his sword and walking toward her. She struggled to rise as he lifted the sword overhead.

"Sorry kid," he said with a smirk. "I guess we're just not nice people, huh?"

Then the smirk was replaced with an almost apologetic expression. Jenn looked, confused, at the red stain that was spreading across the front of his shirt. In the center, the tip of a rapier protruded from Erik's chest.

Nakor pulled his rapier from Erik's body, which fell to the ground with a thud. Then he turned to see Jaimus approaching, wielding his enormous axe.

Taking a swift step backward, Nakor looked at Galadrion. "Yours," he offered.

She stepped forward, into the path of the oncoming axe. Jaimus grinned as the tremendous force of his blow sent Galadrion tumbling to the ground. The grin vanished as she stood up, unharmed.

Reaching both arms over her head, Galadrion leaned back and stretched her shoulder muscles. "That was a good one," she admitted. Then a slow smile spread across her face. "My turn."

Ducking under the next swing, Galadrion locked her fists together and brought them crashing into Jaimus's jaw.

> It's the patented William-Shatner-from-Star-Trek style of double-fisted combat!

Whoo whistled in appreciation as Jaimus flew a good ten feet through the air. He landed in a crumpled heap, quite unconscious.

> A blow to the head sent him flying ten feet? He ain't unconscious. That dude is Dead.

Jenn watched all of this without moving. Then, while Galadrion was leaning over Jaimus's body, she stood up to try and sneak away.

As she stood, Jenn heard a high-pitched buzzing, followed by a thud. Looking down in amazement, she saw that a small arrow now pinned the sleeve of her shirt to the tree behind her.

Whoo shot twice more for good measure. Hopefully, the girl would now be too intimidated to try and run off. If not, it would still take her a minute to tear herself free of the three arrows.

Galadrion knelt and lifted Jaimus's bulky body from the ground. Without saying anything, wordlessly, she walked away, vanishing among the trees.

> "Without saying anything, wordlessly..." Let's all take a moment to appreciate that fine word-craft, shall we?

After watching her go, Nakor turned and walked up to Jenn. He studied the drying blood on her chin and the bruise that was beginning to form under her left eye. She flinched as he reached toward her.

Plucking the three arrows from the tree, Nakor tossed them to the ground. Then he placed a hand on the side of Jenn's face.

Jenn winced. It stung where this man touched her, where Jaimus had hit her. Then she began to relax, for there was a soft warmth to his touch. She could feel the pain in her face beginning to fade.

Once the last traces of Jenn's injuries were gone, Nakor removed his hand and stepped back.

She looked around warily. Keeping her eyes on Nakor, she slowly walked over to retrieve her dagger. It was laying among the undergrowth, next to Erik's body. She stopped, studying the corpse that seemed so out of place among the green ferns.

> That should be "lying," not "laying." Though to be fair to 1995 me, I still have to look up the dif-ference sometimes when I'm writing.

Drawing a foot back, Jenn kicked the body viciously in the side. Angrily, she bent and grabbed her knife.

"Where's Jaimus?" she demanded, turning to Nakor.

Nakor looked to where Galadrion had disappeared.

"Dead," he answered.

"Good!" Jenn answered. She knelt and began searching Erik's body, taking a small pouch of gold and stripping the rings from his hands. Once she was done, she spat on the body for good measure.

Nakor watched impassively. When she had finished, she stood and glared at him defiantly, daring him to say anything.

"Thank you," he said. "That will make it look less suspicious."

Jenn was truly confused. She couldn't understand what these people wanted. She had tried to steal from them, and been caught. But then they had let her escape. Apparently, they had only wanted her to lead them to her companions. Like a fool, she had done just that.

But now what? What did they want with her? The one in purple had healed her face. Why? He hadn't gotten angry with her when she kicked Erik's body. Come to think of it, none of these people seemed to be angry at her at all.

Then the reality of the situation began to sink in. Jaimus and Erik were dead. She was in the middle of the woods, and she was alone. While Jenn was an excellent thief, she knew next to nothing about surviving in the wilderness. Erik had always taken care of providing food and shelter, while Jaimus had provided protection. She was alone, miles from the nearest city. The crude hut they had been living in for the past few months only had enough food for a day or two. After that, Jenn would starve.

Suddenly Jenn was frightened. She looked at the elf in front of her who stood patiently, waiting for her to speak. Disgusted with herself for her fear, Jenn grew angry.

"What do you want?" she yelled.

Nakor smiled sadly. "Nothing," he answered.

Galadrion approached them both silently, looking drained. Nakor sighed, knowing that Jaimus was now a bloodless corpse, his decapitated body lying somewhere in the woods.

> She looks drained? Hey, you should see the other guy! Thank you, thank you, I'm here all week.

It had taken a long time before Nakor was able to accept Galadrion's need to drink the blood of others. After a while, he had learned that without blood, Galadrion would eventually wither away and die. It was something out of her control, a driving instinct which she had no choice but to obey.

It was rare for vampires to be able to control that instinct even to the degree which Galadrion did. She was able to avoid hurting those few whom she considered friends. Nakor had also learned that the disgust of normal people at the habits of vampires was nothing compared to the revulsion Galadrion had for herself. She hated being a vampire with a passion. Only a strong need to survive had prevented her from killing herself years ago.

Seemingly intimidated by Galadrion, Jenn backed away. Then, without warning, she spun and ran off, vanishing into the distance.

After she left, Whoo reappeared. "So much for remaining subtle."

"Well what were we supposed to do?" Pynne asked, materializing next to him. "We couldn't just leave her alone in the woods. We had to follow."

"I know that," Whoo said, sounding irritated. "But this is going to make it easier for someone to track us."

"Hm..." he said sarcastically, bending over to study the ground. "Judging by all the dead bodies, I'd say someone was here recently!"

Pynne rolled her eyes at Whoo's performance. "Go get your arrows."

As Whoo flew to retrieve the three arrows he had used, Nakor tapped Pynne on the shoulder. After a quick whispered exchange, she vanished.

Whoo turned around, inspecting the arrows one at a time and replacing them in his quiver. "Where'd Pynne go?" he asked.

Nakor nodded in the direction Jenn had run. Then he turned to Galadrion.

"Are you ready?" he asked softly.

She nodded.

Whoo faded out of sight once more, and they resumed their journey to Nakor's home.

> I don't remember why exactly they're going back to Nakor's home as opposed to going…well, pretty much *anywhere else in the world*. But I'm sure I had a good reason!

Jenn swore to herself as she stumbled over a tree root. She looked ahead, making sure that Nakor and his witch companion hadn't noticed. They continued without stopping, and Jenn sighed in relief.

After fleeing from Nakor, Jenn had been forced to face the fact that she didn't know how to escape from the woods. She had thought for a few minutes before deciding that her best chance probably lay in following Nakor, hoping he would lead her to a city. So for the past hour, she had crept along, keeping Nakor and Galadrion in sight and trying not to be noticed.

> It's possible the author may have been projecting just a wee bit of White Knight Syndrome onto his purple-cloaked elf.

Jenn shivered. The sun had finished setting about ten minutes ago. With the sun gone from the sky, heat was quickly vanishing as well. She cursed herself for not stopping to grab supplies from the hut she and the others had been staying in.

Up ahead, Nakor and his friend had stopped. Jenn snuck closer, trying to hear what was being said. Once she was close enough, Jenn huddled down in a ball next to a tree to listen.

"If we light a fire, it will serve as a beacon to anyone trying to find us," the witch was saying.

"We need the heat, Galadrion," Nakor replied.

The witch, Galadrion, shook her head. "Would you rather freeze or be stabbed in your sleep?"

Nakor paused for a moment. "What if we build a fire in a pit? That way the light might not be as visible."

"That might work," Galadrion answered. "But how are you planning to dig this pit? Unless you packed a shovel without me noticing."

Even from a distance, Jenn could see the grin on Nakor's face. He knelt down, placing his hands on the earth. Gradually, the dirt melted away under his fingers, sinking into the ground. Soon, the hole was several feet deep, at which point Nakor stood back up and gestured with one hand.

"Your pit, m'lady."

Galadrion sighed. They took a few minutes to gather deadwood from the forest floor. Then Nakor conjured a small flame to light the fire. The light was still visible, but much less so than an above-ground blaze would have been.

Jenn looked on, enviously, as Nakor stretched out beside the fire, pulling his cloak around himself. Galadrion walked away, gathering more firewood.

Feeling cold and thoroughly miserable, Jenn closed her eyes and tried to sleep. After a minute, she sighed and opened her eyes again. Every time she moved at all, goosebumps raced across her flesh. Sleep was not going to come easy this night.

> This kid is a hardened thief and killer who's been
> living with thugs for years. She has a hut where
> she's been staying. And yet the only thing she
> can do is shiver in the cold and look longingly at
> Our Heroes and their fire. Clearly this book was
> written before the discovery of consistent char-
> acterization.

"They're not bad people, you know."

Jenn jumped up, her dagger instantly ready. She looked around, trying to find the source of the voice.

"Put that away, I'm not going to hurt you."

Uncertain now, Jenn hesitantly returned the dagger to its sheath. "Who are you?" she demanded.

A small being, barely three feet tall, appeared in front of her. It was a female, with thin pointed ears and long silver hair. But the most remarkable thing to Jenn was the pair of large, moth-like wings that spouted from the woman's back. "My name's Pynne."

Jenn just sat there, wary of this woman who could appear and disappear at will. She had little experience with magic, and it tended to frighten her.

"Nakor and Galadrion," Pynne continued, "They're nice people. I'm sure they wouldn't mind if you shared their fire."

With an ironic grin, Jenn said "You weren't aware, then, that I tried to rob them?"

Pynne rolled her eyes. "Yeah, I know. I was there. Remember those invisible spirits?"

Jenn's eyes narrowed as she realized what Pynne was saying. She was young enough to be extremely sensitive about being embarrassed. "You tricked me!" she accused angrily.

"Well, technically Whoo started it. He was the one who spotted you taking Nakor's pouch."

"Who?" Jenn asked, confused.

"Whoo," Pynne clarified with a grin. "He's a friend of mine. Another pixie, like me."

Just be glad I didn't try to work in a "Whoo's on first" joke.

Jenn was still suspicious. "What about Galadrion? My knife just bounced off of her. Is she a witch?"

Pynne sighed. "No, Galadrion's not a witch. Galadrion is, well, special. She understands what it's like to be alone," she added.

Jenn's habitual mistrust of others battled against a more basic need, the need for warmth.

"I promise you, you'll be safe."

She looked back, to see Galadrion lying down opposite Nakor. Her chest gradually rose and fell as she slept. Peering closely, she could see the small form of Whoo, also asleep by the fire.

"They're all asleep anyway," Pynne said. "If nothing else, go take a few minutes to thaw yourself out."

The need for warmth won out. Hesitantly, Jenn walked up to the fire, followed closely by Pynne. Timidly, she knelt down, holding out her hands to warm them. When nobody moved, she sat down, being extremely careful not to make any noise.

Pynne watched in amusement as Jenn slowly allowed herself to lay down in front of the fire. She relaxed visibly as the warmth began to thaw her frozen body. Within minutes, she was asleep. Pynne chuckled quietly to herself, then flew over to land next to Galadrion. "When did you start sleeping?" she whispered in amusement.

Galadrion opened her eyes. "Nakor figured she'd be too afraid if anyone was still awake."

Shaking her head, Pynne settled down to sleep.

CHAPTER FIVE

JENN OPENED HER EYES. CONFUSED, SHE TOSSED ASIDE the purple cloak that was covering her. As the memories of last night came back, she sat up and looked around. Galadrion was gone, and the pixies both continued to sleep soundly. Nakor was sitting on the other side of the fire pit, munching on a small apple as he watched her.

Her dagger was out in an instant.

Nakor put a finger to his lips. "Quietly," he whispered, nodding at the sleeping pair, "they've had a rough couple of days."

"I just wanted to get warm," Jenn whispered back. "That's all." Realizing where the cloak had come from, she tossed it to Nakor. He grinned, and set it to one side.

"Want an apple?" he asked, taking one of the small red fruits from a pile at his side. Without waiting for an answer, he threw it at her.

Instinctively, she brought up a hand to catch it. Without taking her eyes off of Nakor, she took a bite.

"They're a little overripe," Nakor commented, finishing

his apple. "In another few weeks, they'll all be gone." He tossed the core into the woods and grabbed another apple.

It was then that Galadrion returned. She was using Nakor's backpack to carry the berries she had gathered. Carefully, she placed the pack between Nakor and Jenn, then backed away and sat down.

Jenn looked warily at Nakor. Hesitantly, she moved closer and warily began to nibble the wild blackberries Galadrion had provided.

> Today we shall eat nothing but FRUIT! Because nothing ruins an epic battle for the fate of the world like constipation.

Nakor looked back at Jenn. "What do you think," he asked, "is it time to wake the pixies?"

Unsure of what to say, Jenn just stared at him.

"Pynne was out late last night," he continued, "so we'll be nice to her." He picked up a berry and bounced it off the back of Pynne's head.

Instantly, she vanished. A moment later, one of the apples floated into the air and launched itself at Nakor, who ducked aside with a grin.

"I thought you were going to be nice to her," Jenn said, confused.

"That's right," Nakor replied. "She gets to wake up Whoo."

Pynne reappeared and flew over to Whoo, pausing once to glare at Nakor. Stopping a few feet away, she began to move her hands in an odd pattern.

Jenn's eyes widened as the largest dog she had ever seen materialized in front of Whoo. It was five feet tall at the shoulder, covered in short, bristling black hair. It had huge white teeth, and glowing red eyes.

She looked at Nakor and Galadrion, who were watching contentedly. "Pynne's an illusionist," Nakor whispered.

Nodding as if this explained everything, Jenn turned

back to watch.

The dog knelt down in front of Whoo. Moving forward until its nose was mere inches from Whoo's ear, it let out a quiet growl.

Whoo stirred. Muttering something incomprehensible, he opened his eyes and turned to stare directly into the mouth of the dog. Letting out a high pitched yelp, he disappeared.

Pynne giggled. The dog stuck out its tongue in an astonishingly human expression, then vanished.

Jenn laughed once. Then, as if frightened by her own outburst, she became silent.

A moment later, Whoo appeared again by the pile of fruit. As if nothing had happened, he calmly started munching on some berries.

Pynne looked over at Jenn. "As you've probably gathered, that's Whoo," she said, pointing.

Jenn nodded.

"And you've already met Nakor and Galadrion," Pynne continued. "I told you they were safe."

She leaned closer to whisper in Jenn's ear. "Honestly, most of the time they're not bright enough to be dangerous."

Jenn grinned in spite of herself. She was still uncomfortable with Galadrion, but she was beginning to like this small pixie.

Pynne started to say more, but stopped. She looked over at Galadrion, who stood up suddenly. Cocking her head, she said "Someone's coming."

Instantly the pixies were gone. "If anything happens, try and hide somewhere." Nakor said, looking at Jenn.

Then he glanced at his cloak, still lying in a pile by his side. Thinking quickly, he kicked it into the fire pit. Then he dumped the berries after it, hoping to conceal the purple cloth that would be a sign to anyone searching for him.

> "Nothing suspicious here! Just an elf out for a leisurely cloak-and-berry burning."

"Pynne," he hissed, "I need a black cloak now!"

> A number of editors would mark me down for that last line. Because how does one "hiss" the word "Pynne," exactly?

Instantly, he was garbed in a heavy black cloak, similar to his purple one. Nakor grabbed the hood and pulled it over his head, concealing his face.

Galadrion had just finished kicking ashes over Nakor's cloak when they heard the voices.

"I told you I saw something out here last night."

"Okay, fine," said a second voice. "so you saw something. We still don't know who they are."

At that point, they emerged into the small clearing. They both looked like mercenaries, probably from the same group that had been at the temple earlier.

"You were supposed to get here last night," Nakor hissed angrily before either of the men could speak.

> This time there's at least a few "S" sounds in his hissing.

The two men stopped, taken aback. The larger of the pair, a tall man with a black beard, stepped forward. Trying to gain control of the exchange, he said "We're looking for an elf and a woman."

Nakor rolled his eyes. "Don't you think I know that? Why do you think Olara stationed us in the woods to begin with?"

Confused, the second man stepped forward. "You were stationed here by Olara?"

Nakor looked at Galadrion, a pained expression on his face. "What kind of fools had Olara started hiring?" he demanded. Galadrion shrugged in response.

"The woman is supposed to be a demon of some sort," the bearded man said. "How do we know that's not her?" He pointed at Galadrion as he spoke.

"For that matter, how do we know you're not an elf?"

Whipping his hood down, Nakor stepped forward. "Of course I'm an elf. Half of Olara's priests are elves, you fool!"

Swallowing hard, he asked "You're one of Olara's priests?"

Nakor's eyes narrowed. "That's right, and this woman is one of her more talented wizards." He turned to Galadrion. "Pass the nice man an apple, would you?"

Whoo, picking up the cue, grabbed an apple and threw it at the man, who grunted as it bounced off his chest.

"Now who are you supposed to be?" Nakor demanded angrily. "You obviously weren't sent to relieve us." He turned to mutter to Galadrion. "Olara probably just decided to leave us here. If this is the kind of help she's got, I don't blame her."

Suddenly the bearded man peered suspiciously at Jenn. "And who is this supposed to be?"

"I caught her trying to pick my pocket," answered Nakor. Galadrion raised an eyebrow at that, but said nothing.

Raised eyebrow count: 11

"I figured we'd sell her to someone as a kitchen slave or something," Nakor continued. "We're not getting paid enough to make a decent living anyway."

The man laughed at that. "Ain't that the truth." He continued to study Jenn for a moment. "My name's Lucas. That blond fellow over there's Stephan."

This is the part where they bond over low wages

and jokes about slavery.

The mercenary identified as Stephan still seemed suspicious. "If she's your prisoner, why isn't she tied up?"

Nakor laughed harshly. "Aside from the fact that Galadrion here would kill her before she got anywhere, just where exactly do you think she'd go if she escaped?"

Lucas joined in the laughter. "Stephan's just bitter 'cause he thought we'd found those two we were looking for."

Looking slightly sheepish, Stephan wandered a few steps away. Then he turned around and said "What were you're names again?"

"Thomas," Nakor replied without missing a beat. "The sorceress is Lauren."

Lucas clapped Nakor on the shoulder. "It's great to meet another underpaid mercenary."

Stephan stopped and stared at Nakor. "I thought you were a priest."

What happened next was over so quickly that Jenn had to replay the events in her mind. Nakor shoved Lucas into Galadrion, who snapped his neck before he knew what was happening. Stephan managed to get his sword partly drawn before an arrow slammed into his chest, followed closely by another. Within seconds, both men lay dead.

"Oops," Nakor said, looking embarrassed. "I think I made a mistake." His black cloak faded into nothingness as Pynne ended her illusion.

"They needed killing anyway," Galadrion commented. "Otherwise what would you have done with them?"

> These characters are much more cavalier about killing than I remember. I was a bloodthirsty little college student back in 1995…

Pynne reappeared, glaring at Nakor. "Next time, you be the sorcerer and let one of us to the talking."

> Or maybe "do the talking"? This is why copy-
> editors are so important.

Jenn just watched in amazement. It had been the most efficient killing she had ever seen in her life. "Not bright enough to be dangerous?" she whispered quietly.

Bending down, Nakor retrieved his cloak from the fire pit. He stepped away and shook it violently, sending ashes and berries in all directions. He looked sadly at the berry stains and burn marks.

"It would make you too easy to identify," Whoo commented as he reappeared.

"I know," Nakor answered sadly. "But it was so comfortable."

Dropping the cloak in the dirt, he turned to Jenn. "There are some people who don't like me very much."

She looked at the two bodies.

"You're probably going to be safer if you don't follow," Nakor continued without stopping.

"So what will they do if they find out I was with you?" Jenn demanded.

Nakor closed his eyes. He knew what would happen. Olara or one of her priests would ask questions, trying to find out what she knew. After that, she would be killed. He looked helplessly at Galadrion.

"She might be safer with us," Galadrion offered.

"It will take another half a day to get back to my home," Nakor said. "Why don't you come with us until then, and we can tell you the whole story. Then you can decide what you want to do."

Jenn considered this. Alone, she would probably starve, or be captured by the people following Nakor. "Can you get me to a city?" she asked.

"There's a small town about a mile past my house," Nakor answered.

"Okay. Then let's go," Jenn said impatiently.

Nakor smiled, and they resumed their march.

"And her sword can drain people's blood?" Jenn asked for the third time.

"Both the sword and the dagger can, yes," Nakor answered. Jenn had been fascinated by the idea of long-dead gods and powerful spells. For hours, she had alternated between listening silently to Nakor's tale, and assaulting him with a barrage of questions.

"And the coin protects her from finding you?"

"As long as we stay within fifty paces of Galadrion, yes."

"Then why didn't she find us this morning when Galadrion was off gathering berries."

Nakor hesitated. He looked at Galadrion.

"I stayed within fifty paces," she said with a shrug.

"Oh," Jenn said.

Gesturing for silence, Nakor knelt down. "The forest thins out very quickly up ahead. After that, we'll come to a river. The castle is just beyond."

"You live in a castle?" Jenn demanded.

"Well, it's not much of a castle," Nakor admitted.

Cautiously, they crept up to the very edge of the woods. From there they could see crumbled ruins of the castle in the distance.

"I see four of Olara's mercenaries," Nakor whispered.

"There's a priest over there," Galadrion pointed, "standing in the shadows."

I still don't remember why they came back here.

"So," Pynne asked, "All we need to do is get across the river, get inside the castle, get supplies, and get back out without anyone spotting us?"

Aha! They need supplies! Which apparently

> aren't available anywhere else in this world. Un-
> derstandable, since my worldbuilding thus far
> seems to lack any sort of shops, towns, settle-
> ments, or communities.

"That's right," Nakor answered. "And I don't have the slightest idea how to do it."

Pynne turned to Whoo, and they whispered back and forth for a moment. Then they both vanished.

"Wait here," came Pynne's voice. "You'll know when to move."

Nakor looked at Galadrion and Jenn. Shrugging, he sat down to wait.

"The nearest town is a mile downriver," he said, turning to Jenn.

> So there *is* a town! But we can't go there for
> supplies, because…um…

Jenn looked down. Despite her initial distrust, she had begun to like these people. They were the first people she had ever met that didn't seem to want anything from her. Besides, she was fascinated by Nakor's tales of magic and evil goddesses. While she was a long way from actually trusting any of them, there was still a strong urge to remain with this odd group of people.

"I don't know," she said. "Do you really think I'd be safe there?"

Nakor looked at Galadrion. "I'm not sure," he answered. "Olara probably doesn't even know that you've seen us, so there would be no reason for them to bother you."

"Still," Jenn said, considering, "I think I might be safer with you than I would be on my own."

"How do you know you're safe with us?" asked Galadrion.

That made Jenn pause. She was still confused about

Galadrion, but she had also begun to admire her. The image of this tall woman casually snapping Lucas's neck had burned itself into her memory. "I'd be safe," she concluded.

> Every young girl should have a tormented bloodsucking killer to look up to.

Nakor's first instinct was to send her away in order to protect her. But he had long ago learned the futility of trying to force his decisions on other people. If this was what Jenn wanted, he would have to respect that.

"Are you sure this is what you want?" he asked sadly.

Jenn nodded.

A ways down the river, a purple-cloaked Nakor peeked out of the forest and began making his way toward the castle. Pynne frowned. She gestured once, and Nakor's brown boots shimmered briefly, then turned black. "Much better," she muttered.

> Once again, transitions are for the WEAK!

It wasn't long before one of the guards spotted Pynne's illusion. With a shout, he drew his sword and began running.

"Stay here," the priest directed two of the men. He and the two hired guards began to chase after Nakor. Soon, they had vanished into the forest.

The two men who stayed behind turned to look at each other.

"Great," said one, "So much for either of us getting the extra fifty gold."

"Wasn't there supposed to be a woman with him?" asked the other.

"Yeah. But there wasn't any reward for getting her."

His companion leered. "You mean we aren't getting paid any reward for her. I think we could find ways of making it profitable."

The other man laughed.

> Ugh. No fantasy novel is complete without some sort of rape threat. Okay, look. Because I am disgusted with my 1995 self for thoughtlessly adding this particular cliché, I say we pretend the two bad guys are planning to turn a profit by asking Galadrion to teach them her wicked embroidery skills, after which they hope to start a business selling tablecloths.

Whoo was beginning to grow irritated with the conversation. Perching on the remains of what was once a wall, he carefully strung his bow.

Nakor watched as one of the two guards jerked back, clutching his throat. The other swiftly followed.

> Oh no! The bad guys' embroidery dream has come to a sad and sudden end.

He looked at his companions. "Teamwork," he commented. As one, the trio raced up to the river.

There had been a sturdy wooden bridge that spanned the river. Now, all that remained were two posts on either bank where Nakor had anchored the bridge.

"Apparently they don't want to make it easy for us," Nakor commented. With that, he slipped off his boots and prepared to swim across.

Galadrion grabbed his arm. "Nakor, I can't cross that," she said, looking at the deep water ahead.

Nakor and Jenn looked at her.

"You can't cross running water?" Nakor asked, remembering something he had once heard about vampires.

Galadrion rolled her eyes. "I can't swim."

> I kind of like that reversal of expectations there.

With a laugh, Nakor turned back to the river. Closing his eyes, he concentrated on the water. His brow wrinkled. Water was not the easiest of the elements to manipulate.

After a short time, he opened his eyes. A bridge of ice stood where Nakor had frozen a strip of the water. "After you, Galadrion," he said gallantly.

> Nakor's magic can do *anything* the plot requires!

"You just want me to be the one to fall through if your bridge isn't strong enough," she accused. But she led them across to the castle anyway.

There, Nakor found that the heavy oaken door had been smashed. With a sigh, he led the others inside. Whoo followed, after taking a moment to unstring his bow.

> Whoo read ahead and knew there was nobody else lurking inside, so there's no need for weapons. He's clever that way.

Once inside, Nakor moved swiftly. He opened a small door, then gave a quiet prayer of thanks. Olara's men had been so busy trying to find him that they hadn't bothered to steal anything.

He grabbed a coil of rope and shoved it in his backpack. As he grabbed other assorted supplies, he took a moment to glance back at Jenn.

> Thank the gods! There's nowhere else we possibly could have gone for *rope*.

"Do you need anything?"

Surprised, she shook her head. Nakor turned back and grabbed a few other items, then shut the door. Then he pursed his lips and whistled loudly.

A moment later, there was a flapping of wings as Flame flew out of another room to land on his shoulder.

"Wonder where he's been hiding?" Galadrion said.

> Wherever all good characters go when the author forgets about them for a few chapters. Also, the whole whistling thing? They really aren't worried about the remaining bad guys that ran off after illusory Nakor, are they?

"There are plenty of good hiding places around here," Nakor answered, ruffling Flame's feathers. "Lots of good mice," he added with a grin.

"Yeah, they ate most of your food while we were away," Galadrion commented. "I grabbed what was left, though."

"Great," Nakor said. He grabbed some leather cord from his pack and cut off a small piece. He used that to tie his blond hair back into a long braid.

> The elf's tying his hair back. It's on, now!

Reaching into a closet and pulled out a long brown cloak and tossed it over his shoulders.

> Wait, what?

"How do I look?" he asked once he fastened the cloak shut.

Galadrion raised an eyebrow.

> Raised eyebrow count: 12

"It's the best I can do for a disguise," he said defensively.

Moving quickly, they left the castle. Galadrion and Nakor each grabbed one of the dead guards, dumping them in the river as they re-crossed the bridge of ice. Once they reached the other side, Nakor stopped and looked back at the river. He waved his hand, and there was a loud cracking sound. Slowly, the ice bridge began to break apart and float downriver, melting as it went.

"Pynne said she'd meet us at the tree you fell out of," Whoo said as they ran.

"Tree you fell out of?" asked Galadrion.

> It pains me to read Galadrion's line with no re-
> sponse from anyone. It's like she went for a high
> five, and the rest of the party just left her hang-
> ing.

Pynne flew swiftly through the woods, sending her phantom Nakor darting between the trees. She paused to glance behind, making sure the others were still following. Seeing the three men crashing through the undergrowth, she began moving again.

To the right she could hear the river flowing. It had been about five minutes since she first started this chase. She figured Nakor and the others would need at least another ten.

> Pynne has a digital watch for keeping track of
> time so precisely. It's a pixie thing.

She ducked, narrowly avoiding a large tree branch. It was becoming more difficult to fly and maintain her illusion at the same time.

Breathing heavily now, she continued to lead the men further from the castle. They were slowly beginning to gain, as she was unable to fly at her usual rate.

Worried, Pynne looked around for some way of prolonging the chase. Perhaps there would be some sort of rough terrain over which she could lead them. If not, they would soon catch up to her illusion. Once that happened, Pynne didn't know what she would do.

As she flew, she passed two baby bears playing under the

close supervision of their mother. Pynne grinned briefly, remembering Nakor's story about the bear family he had disrupted.

To the right lay the river. Up ahead, the forest seemed to stretch on forever. It was the most obliging forest Pynne had ever seen. Nice, even ground with trees spaced far enough apart to allow for easy movement among them. Nothing seemed to offer a promising route to prolong the chase.

"Maybe I could send them into the river," she muttered to herself. It wasn't a very promising idea, but it was the only thing she could think of to keep her pursuers occupied.

Suddenly she had an idea. She concentrated, and Nakor began to veer to the left, coming around in a wide circle.

Minutes later, she dropped the illusion and landed gracefully on a high tree branch.

"He disappeared behind those bushes!" the priest called to his men.

Putting on an extra burst of speed, the three men crashed through the bushes, then came to an abrupt halt. Nakor was nowhere to be seen. Up ahead, two tiny bears peered curiously at these intruders. They looked around nervously.

"He's supposed to be a wizard or something, right?" asked one of the mercenaries.

"Maybe he changed into one of the bears," offered the other.

"Can he do that?" asked the first.

"Well he couldn't just vanish!" insisted the priest. "Spread out, and start..."

He was interrupted by a loud growling from behind. As one, they turned around to see the mother bear rear up to her full height of nine feet. Angrily, the mother bear advanced, seeking to protect its young.

Pynne flew back in the direction she had come. She

winced sympathetically, hearing the first scream from behind her.

"Silly footerlings."

And they all shared a hearty chuckle as their enemies were mauled and mutilated by an angry bear.

CHAPTER SIX

NAKOR JUMPED, STARTLED, AS A SMALL PINECONE bounced off his head.

"That's for this morning," Pynne commented, coming into view in front of him.

"What happened to the others?" asked Whoo.

"Well," Pynne started, "the bear had the advantage of surprise, so they probably didn't do too well."

She landed on the ground and folded her wings behind her. "Never get between a mother and her young," she commented to herself.

"Has anyone ever told you that you have a mean streak?" asked Nakor.

Pynne grinned. Then she studied him closely for a moment. "I liked the other cloak better."

"Me too," Nakor said.

"So now what?" Whoo asked.

"I think we should try and find the scroll Thomas was talking about," Nakor commented.

> You think? I didn't write all of that exposition and plot-bait for nothing, you know!

"You don't even know if that exists," Pynne protested. "And even if it does, all he said was that it was 'safe from her.' How are we supposed to find it?"

"In the temple," Jenn said quietly, without looking up.

Everyone stared at her. "Beg your pardon?" Whoo said.

Jenn looked at Nakor. "You said Olara couldn't stay inside the temple, right?"

Suddenly an enormous grin spread across Nakor's face. "Right," he answered.

Jenn shifted position, uncomfortable at being the center of attention. "So what better place to hide something from her?"

"I don't suppose you could tell us where inside the temple Averlon would have hidden it?" asked Whoo.

Jenn shook her head.

Something was tugging at the back of Nakor's mind. It felt as if there was some fact he was forgetting, some little bit of information he was overlooking. He closed his eyes, trying to remember.

"I guess we could just explore the whole thing," Pynne said. "How big can a temple be, anyway?"

"They were in there exploring for several days," Galadrion commented.

"So how many days are we going to have to spend looking for this thing, once we get to the temple?" Whoo asked.

Pynne turned to look at Nakor. "I don't suppose you could narrow down where in the temple this scroll might be hidden?"

Nakor's eyes widened. "Not in the temple, underneath it."

"Excuse me?" asked Pynne.

He turned excitedly to Galadrion. "Do you remember

when I was talking about the dreams I had last night? The ones where I was back in the temple?"

Galadrion nodded.

"The events in my dream really happened, two years ago," he continued. "I was wounded by skeletons, and crawled off into a hidden room to heal the wound in my side."

He looked around. "Your point being..." Whoo ventured.

"Magic doesn't work in Olara's temple."

Comprehension dawned on Galadrion. "You cast a healing spell, and it worked!"

"Which means I wasn't in the temple anymore, or else I couldn't have healed myself." Nakor finished.

He beamed at Jenn. "You were right, the temple would keep Olara from finding the scroll. But her priests could still go in and out of the temple, and so they would have found it years ago. Unless it was somewhere secret, someplace you need to go *through* the temple to find."

"That room I stumbled into was designed to be hidden. I bet even Olara doesn't know it's there. And there were other doors leading out of the room. So there are probably some underground tunnels that aren't a part of Olara's temple."

"The temple would keep Olara from getting to those tunnels. By making them secret, it would keep her priests from finding them as well. If Averlon hid his scroll anywhere in the temple, that's where it would be."

"So let's get to the temple, find the scroll, and finish this whole mess!" said Whoo impatiently.

"Where is this temple at?" asked Jenn.

Nakor pointed at the mountains in the west. "There's a cliff about a hundred or so miles from here. Olara's temple is built into that cliff."

"We can get horses in town." He looked at Jenn. "Can you ride?"

"Ride? As in a horse?" she asked dubiously.

"Don't worry, it's easy," Nakor said with a grin.

Jenn just looked at him.

"You want three horses now? On such short notice?" the dealer demanded, looking pained.

"That's correct," answered Nakor.

"Alas, you have come at a bad time for Abu-Jaheem," said the horse dealer. "I used to be the most famous dealer of horses this side of the Serpent Mountains." He shook his head sadly. "My customers have swindled me, taken advantage of my kind-hearted nature, until now I am left with next to nothing. Every day my family lives in fear of starvation."

> I'm sorry. Someone bring me a TARDIS. I'm going back in time to smack the stupid out of 1995 Jim.

"Saddles too," added Nakor.

Abu-Jaheem stared at him. "These horses are all that I have, my only means to survive. Surely you can understand that. I could not bear to part with three of them for less than..."

His voice trailed off as Nakor drew his rapier.

"There is no need for that, kind sir!" Abu-Jaheem said, backing away.

Handing the sword to Galadrion, Nakor took the scabbard and held it upside down over his hand. He shook it once, and a small, thin leather packet slid into his hand. Nakor carefully unrolled the packet and selected a pair of small red rubies from among the gleaming gems. He held the jewels up to the light, then handed them to the horse dealer.

"I don't have time to bargain," Nakor said, rolling the remaining gems back into a tight bundle. He slid the gems back into the scabbard, followed by his rapier.

Nakor glanced up to see Galadrion and Jenn staring at him. "I figure it's safest this way. You never know when someone will try to pick your pocket."

Jenn rolled her eyes.

"Where did you get that kind of money?" Galadrion asked.

"Here and there," he answered evasively. "After a hundred and twenty seven years, money starts to add up."

"A hundred and twenty seven years?" Jenn demanded.

Nakor grinned and tapped a pointed ear with one finger. "One of the advantages of being an elf."

> "We also have a great dental plan."

Within minutes, they sat upon three of Abu-Jaheem's horses, complete with saddles and a two-day supply of grain.

"You have the thanks of Lucas Stephanson," Nakor called back as they rode into the forest.

"Lucas Stephanson?" Galadrion asked from her horse.

"First thing that came to mind," Nakor replied with a shrug. "Besides, it might confuse anyone who tries to follow us."

Whoo sat comfortably behind him, grasping Nakor's cloak with one hand to keep his balance.

There was a shout, followed by a thump behind them. Nakor vaulted from the saddle and walked over to where Jenn had fallen. "You okay?" he asked.

"The stupid thing stopped suddenly," Jenn replied sullenly. "I told you I couldn't ride."

Nakor grinned. "You took that fall without getting banged up too badly," he observed. "That's the first step in becoming a good rider."

> On a related note, I think for many of us, the first step in becoming a good writer is to write crap. In all seriousness, none of us are born

> knowing how to write. Almost all of us will pro-
> duce a lot of really lousy stories before we start
> to get good. (Not all of us will choose to publish
> those lousy stories, but that's a whole separate
> discussion...)

He studied the saddle briefly. "First of all, let's get this saddle adjusted properly." Nakor took a moment to shorten the stirrups. "That should help you keep your balance a little better."

He walked up to the horse. After casting a quick spell, he whispered something into the horse's ear. Its eyes widened, and its ears flicked back. Nakor just stepped away and raised an eyebrow at the horse.

> Raised eyebrow count: 13. Now we're raising
> eyebrows at horses?

"I think it should be okay now," he said to Jenn. Making a basket with his hands, he boosted her up onto the saddle. Turning, Nakor returned to his own mount.

As they trotted onward, Pynne flew down to hover alongside Nakor. "What did you say to that horse?" she asked.

"I just told him how important it was that we make it to the temple as quickly as possible," Nakor replied innocently. "I also mentioned what would happen to anyone, horses included, that got in the way of that goal."

> Nakor really is a bit of an a-hole, isn't he.

Pynne looked back at Jenn's horse. The animal seemed to be stepping very carefully now, turning his head from time to time to check on his rider.

"I think things should be a bit smoother from now on," Nakor said with a grin.

The next day, Pynne peered down at a group of men

who sat around a campfire, chatting idly among themselves. Once they had gotten away from the town, Galadrion had suggested someone scout ahead to make sure they didn't run into any unpleasant surprises.

Pynne and Whoo had both volunteered. With their ability to fly and become invisible, they were ideal for looking around without being detected. Furthermore, as far as anyone knew, Nakor only had one travelling companion. The only people who knew about Jenn or the pixies were either safe in Thomas's temple or dead.

> Assuming those bad guys at the temple haven't gotten in and killed everyone there. This whole book has a bit of an "Out of sight, out of mind" thing going on.

Whoo had taken the first day, flying about a mile ahead of the others and reporting back every few hours. It had been remarkably uneventful. Boring was the word he had used.

Only an hour after setting out this morning, Pynne had overtaken a group of travellers. A few of the men rode in a horse-drawn wagon, while the rest sat astride horses, surrounding the wagon.

Immediately after finding them, Pynne had flown back to inform the others. Once that was done, she quickly returned to the small band and had been watching them ever since.

A few minutes ago, they had stopped for lunch. For the first time, Pynne was able to see everyone clearly. Fourteen of them, mostly men. There were a few women, too. They must have been riding in the wagon, Pynne concluded.

She landed on a branch, almost directly over the campfire. Her wings were sore from flying back and forth with such urgency, and she welcomed the chance to rest her aching muscles.

Pynne waited quietly, only half listening as the group

chatted idly about the food and other everyday matters. Suddenly she sat upright, hoping her ears had misunderstood what was just said.

"What was that?" asked one of the men, echoing Pynne's thoughts.

"I said, I wonder what this 'City of the Spider' is going to be like?" the speaker repeated. "If you'd stop cramming that lamb down your throat like a starved beggar, you would have heard me the first time."

> Of course these random travelers on the road just happen to be connected to Nakor's quest. The way the worldbuilding is going, nothing outside of Nakor's quest exists at all. If you drew a map of the world, it would literally be the routes he and his companions took and the places they stopped. The rest of the page would be blank.

Someone leaned forward intently. "I know what it's like," he said in a quiet tone.

"And just how would you know that, Howard Barkett?"

"I talked to Morselas."

Instantly, the group was quiet. "You talked to the elf priest?" a woman asked, awestruck.

"You did not," said the man who had asked the question to begin with. He turned to the others. "Only moved here a few months ago and he's already trying to impress Melanie over there," he added, pointing.

A few of the men laughed, but most of them were still intent on hearing what Howard had to say.

"Morselas has been in our village for a year now, and nobody has been willing to talk to him," Howard explained. "But now, with him pressuring us to visit Olara in person, I decided it was time to ask some questions."

"He's always been willing to talk about the second coming of Olara, and how she will restore the world to a more pure form. But he always seems to ignore the more mundane details."

"What do you mean?" Melanie asked.

"Why did Morselas come to our village? Are there other priests in other towns, preaching the worship of Olara? What is this marvelous City of the Spiders, of which he speaks so fondly?"

"What did he say?"

Pynne leaned out from her perch, listening.

"He welcomed me into the small hut in which he has lived for the past year. There, he began to speak again of the wonder and power of Olara."

The others nodded, having heard that kind of talk many times before.

> Despite the fact that NOBODY TALKS LIKE THAT!

"At first, he was unwilling to answer my questions. But suddenly, I know not why, he changed his mind and began to talk about Olara's city."

"He said it is centered around the small stone hut in which Calugar the Betrayer first designed the spell to resurrect Olara. For the past two years, her followers have gathered around that point until now there are hundreds, thousands who live there."

"It is a place of great power, alien and primitive. But it is the place where Olara has begun to change the world, to improve it. She is returning everything to its natural state."

"So why does he want us to go there?" someone asked.

"Olara's power grows daily," Howard answered. "But there are many who oppose her in her quest. The journey to her city is one of the final tests of faith that must be endured by her followers. Others, both gods and men, have created obstacles in the hope of weakening our mistress. The forests have begun to grow black and twisted through their efforts. They have spread rumors about Olara, describing her as evil and cruel."

"We are needed to aid her in her efforts. As her following grows, it becomes easier for her to hunt out and destroy these heretics."

> Ever feel like other people only exist to spoon-feed you plot details?

With that, Howard stood up and stretched. "And now, if you'll excuse me," he said to his audience, "I need to go answer a call of nature." Turning, he walked into the forest. Hidden from the others' view, he pulled a necklace out of his shirt. Curious, Pynne followed.

Once he was far enough away, he stopped in front of a tree. Pynne flew up next to him and studied the small talisman his hand. Her eyes widened.

Clutching the small silver spider in one hand, Howard closed his eyes. "Olara, your servant calls."

He cocked his head slightly, as if listening, but Pynne heard nothing.

"They should arrive within a day, mistress."

He paused again. He must be hearing Olara's responses in his mind, Pynne decided.

"No, they suspect nothing. I told them that I needed to go into seclusion for a month of ritual prayer. In this way, Morselas's disappearance will be unnoticed long enough for me to lead this first group to your city. Once they arrive, others from the village will soon follow."

Pynne tensed. This must be Morselas, the elven priest. She closed her eyes and concentrated.

Yes, she could barely detect the presence of the illusion masking his form. Pynne opened her eyes again.

"Yes mistress, I am aware of the problem. Nakor and the vampire," he frowned, as if someone had interrupted him.

"Pixies? He has pixies helping him? And a girl?" He looked confused.

"Ah, a young thief. I see. Thank you, Olara, I shall inform the others." He glanced behind him. "I must go now, before they suspect anything."

Tucking his amulet back into his shirt, Howard walked back to rejoin the others.

Stunned, Pynne just sat on her branch and stared. Olara knew about her and the others. How had anyone managed to learn of their presence? Olara obviously knew Nakor, and Galadrion had been staying with him for long enough for anyone to learn of her. Pynne's brow furrowed as she tried to figure out how this had happened.

A few minutes later, she flew back toward Nakor and the others.

Pynne popped into view between Galadrion and Nakor. She hovered there briefly, out of breath. Sensing something was wrong, they pulled the reins of their horses, coming to a halt. Jenn's horse stopped on his own, Nakor's words from the previous day still echoing in his mind.

"There's a group a few miles up heading towards the 'City of the Spiders.' They're being led by a priest named Morselas."

She looked intently at Nakor. "He knows about Jenn, Whoo, and I."

Nakor closed his eyes. This was the one thing he had hoped to avoid. If nobody knew about the others, it would be easier to keep them relatively safe.

"Do you know how he found out?" he asked.

Pynne shook her head. "He was talking to Olara through his holy amulet. She told him. But I don't know how she learned about us."

"The obvious answer," Galadrion began slowly, "is that we're being spied on."

Nakor nodded his agreement.

Jenn looked around nervously. "So what do we do?"

"Whoo," Nakor began, "could you fly behind us for a while and see if anyone's following?"

With a nod, Whoo vanished.

"Whoever is watching us, they haven't done anything yet," Nakor said. "So we probably aren't in any immediate danger."

"But they probably know where we're going," Pynne pointed out. "Once we get to the temple, there could be hundreds of guards waiting for us. For that matter, how do we know that we won't be ambushed the next time we ride over a hill?"

"We don't," Nakor said. "So it would probably be a good idea for you to keep scouting ahead as we go."

Pynne rolled her eyes. "Whatever would you do without me?" she asked sarcastically. Then she launched herself into the air, fading from sight in mid-leap.

Nakor watched her go, staring off into the distance even after she was gone. Absently, he petted Flame with one finger as he wondered what to make of this new development.

Sighing, he turned to look at Galadrion and Jenn. "Be careful," he said simply. Nudging his horse with his knees, he began to follow Pynne.

Galadrion and Jenn glanced at each other. Turning, they began following Nakor. Galadrion held back, allowing Jenn to get ahead of her. Hopefully, she and Nakor would be able to provide some small measure of protection this way, if necessary.

Somberly, the group rode toward the mountains in the distance.

> Desperately, the readers prayed for variation in sentence structure.

The horses snorted nervously. The mountains were closer now. One peak in particular loomed majestically ahead of them, overshadowing its brothers. But that was not the cause of the horses' discomfort.

"I don't like this," Pynne said nervously.

Whoo had been unable to find anyone following them, and had stayed with the others since returning. Likewise, Pynne had returned, occasionally flying ahead to make sure they didn't overtake Morselas. But something about the area instilled a sense of discomfort, causing her to unconsciously remain close to her companions.

Nakor started. "Hm?" he asked, distracted.

"We don't like this," Whoo said in a loud voice.

For hours now, it had been like this. To Jenn, it felt like the forest had grown angry. She imagined that the trees themselves wanted to reach out and strike her dead. The slightest noise would make them jump.

Nakor closed his eyes. "The land is sick," he muttered, almost to himself. He could sense the disturbance all around him. It permeated the air, the trees, the ground, even the insects that buzzed annoyingly in their ears.

> "The land is sick"? It's like I gobbled up every fantasy cliché I could find, then vomited them onto my word processor. (Word Perfect 6.0, if I remember correctly.)

He looked at the ground. "The leaves are starting to fall," he commented.

"It's the middle of summer," Whoo protested. He could see the thin carpet of dead leaves on the ground as well as the rest of them. But there was a strong urge to deny the existence of the wrongness around them.

Even if it had been the right season for the trees to shed their leaves, he would have known something was wrong. The leaves that had not yet decayed to a crispy brown color were green, as if the tree had been perfectly healthy when it lost its foliage.

"I know," Nakor answered.

There was silence for a few minutes. Eventually, Jenn

spoke up hesitantly.

"What's happening?"

"Everything is dying," Galadrion answered quietly. She had an intimate connection to death, and could feel it surrounding them. For the first time in years, she felt uneasy.

"It's more than that," Nakor said. "It feels...wrong somehow." He frowned. "My magic is closely linked to the natural world. I can feel the energy around us."

He looked at the others. "It feels wrong, distorted," he said, frustrated. "I don't know how to explain it."

> Neither did the author, obviously.

"Olara?" ventured Pynne.

"Probably," Nakor answered. "Thomas said she twists the life around her."

"Morselas said the area around Olara's city had grown black and twisted through the efforts of her enemies," Pynne said. "And that Olara had begun to 'improve' the world, returning it to a more natural state."

"I suspect the land's suffering is due to Olara," Nakor commented. "She probably made up the story about her enemies in order to keep her followers from finding out just what kind of improvements she was making. By the time they learn what Olara is really doing, they'll be too deeply ensnared in her web to protest."

Nobody said anything after that. As they rode on, they began to see visible evidence of the distortion Nakor had described. The trees were now completely bare. A damp, sickly smell hung in the air from the thousands of rotten leaves that covered the earth. There was nothing green to be seen for miles.

Even the trees themselves looked wrong. Branches jutted out at odd angles, and the bark of various trees had begun to take on a dark, uniform shine.

"It's like they're just skeletons of trees," Jenn commented. It was a disturbingly accurate observation.

Nakor's horse abruptly reared in fright. Startled, Flame launched himself from Nakor's shoulders, coming to rest in a nearby tree.

Hitting the ground, Nakor rolled back over one shoulder and came to his feet. Galadrion jumped from her horse and reached over to steady Jenn's mount, preventing it from dislodging her as well. Once Jenn's animal was secure, Galadrion looked up to see what had scared the animals.

About twenty yards ahead, standing in the middle of the path, was a large buck. But it was unlike the proud, beautiful deer they were used to seeing. The buck had obviously been affected by whatever was twisting the forest around them.

It was covered in sleek, glistening black fur. There were a few tufts of brown hair scattered across its body, showing what the buck might have looked like before being affected.

A magnificent pair of antlers jutted from its forehead. Nakor studied the antlers closely, noting the razor sharp edges and the lethal points. They gleamed metallically, looking as if they were made of steel. But the most terrifying thing to see were the eyes.

> Basically, imagine a cross between Bambi and The Punisher.

Madness shone brilliantly from within those wide eyes. Moving slowly, Nakor began to cast a spell, hoping to talk to the creature.

> Madness is very shiny.

The buck leapt forward without warning. Before anyone could react, its sharp antlers stabbed deep into the throat of Nakor's horse.

With a sharp twist of its head, the deer broke the horse's neck. It backed away slowly, freeing its antlers from the dead animal. Once its antlers had been withdrawn, the horse collapsed to the ground with a thud. The buck shook his head violently, sending a shower of blood in all directions.

This was too much for the other horses. Galadrion ripped Jenn from her mount as they turned and raced back down the trail, fleeing.

> As opposed to racing down the trail, doing the Macarena?

The deer looked up, contemplating the escaping beasts.

Crossing his fingers, Nakor began to speak in soft, quiet tones.

The buck glared at him with contempt and snorted once.

Nakor took a step back as the animal began to advance. Noting the tensed muscles, Nakor leapt aside as the deer charged.

"Galadrion?" he called. "Whoo?"

Moving with incredible agility, the deer spun and launched itself at Galadrion. She stepped to one side and grabbed at the animal as it passed by. Jerking her arm back, she cried out and clutched her hand.

The buck stopped suddenly, biting at the small arrow that suddenly protruded from his side. It was joined by another, inches from the first.

Shaking its head in confusion, the deer reared up on its hind legs and kicked wildly. That was when a dagger tumbled through the air to hit it in the chest.

> While it's an interesting visual, I don't think "tumbled" is really the word you want when describing a thrown knife.

The deer fell backward, letting out a high pitched shriek. It flailed about helplessly for a moment. Whoo took that opportunity to shoot it in the throat.

"Stubborn thing, isn't it?" Nakor commented. The deer was still kicking weakly, despite the knife and Whoo's arrows stuck in its body.

Carefully avoiding the sharp hooves, Nakor walked over and slashed the deer's throat with his rapier.

> We're more than halfway through the book. At any point, have you felt any real sense of tension or danger? We've had characters talking about how bad and scary Olara is, and there's been a series of interchangeable, two-dimensional bad guys for Nakor et al. to kill, but the threat doesn't feel genuine. I'm not worried about the characters or the fate of the world, because nothing we've seen has come across as a true, believable danger. Including Serial Killer Bambi there.

With a final kick, it died. Immediately Nakor turned to Galadrion, who was still clutching her hand in shock. His eyes widened as he looked at the hand.

From between her clenched fingers dripped a steady red trickle of blood.

"I grabbed it by the antlers," she explained with a wince. "They sliced into my hand like a razor."

As they watched, the flow of blood gradually slowed, and then stopped. When she opened her hand, only a set of pink scars marked her palm. Over the next few minutes, those too faded away.

Shocked, the others watched wordlessly as she began to wipe her bloodcovered hands on her trousers.

"How?" asked Jenn, confused.

Galadrion turned to look at the dead horse, then at the deer. "I don't know," she replied.

"It's the magic," Nakor commented. "If a powerful enough enchantment is put on a weapon, it would be able to injure you. It seems that our friend the deer has just such an enchantment upon him."

"Why would someone want a deer that could hurt Galadrion?" Whoo asked, confused.

"I doubt anyone would," Nakor answered. "This is probably just a side effect of whatever is happening here."

He looked Galadrion in the eyes. "Be careful."

She nodded.

Jenn walked over to retrieve her dagger from the dead animal. Placing a foot on the body, she wrenched it free.

> The dagger. She's not wrenching her foot off or anything like that. This has been today's lesson in pronoun antecedents.

Whoo, trying to get his arrows out of the body, found himself unable to do so. The tough skin of the deer prevented him from ripping out the barbed arrowhead. Finally, the arrow he was tugging on snapped, causing him to flap his wings madly to keep from falling over backward.

Pynne grinned. "I'm glad your aim is better than your balance."

Whoo ignored her. "If everything in this area is as tough as that deer, we're going to have problems," he observed.

"I doubt everything will be this bad as we go on," Nakor replied.

He stared sadly at the dead horse. "I suspect it will get worse."

> Dang, Nakor. Downer, much?

There was silence for a minute. Then Pynne said "The cliff looks like it's just a few hours away on foot. Let's get going before something else comes along."

Silently, Nakor began to transfer the supplies from the saddlebags of the dead horse to his own pack. "We lost a lot of our food when the other horses bolted," he said.

"So why don't we just find something to eat?" asked Jenn.

Wordlessly, Galadrion picked a berry off a nearby bush. She tossed it to Jenn. "Would you like to eat something like that?"

Jenn studied the small berry. It was dry and shriveled, looking like a seed with wrinkled black skin. There was some resemblance to a raisin, but this berry was as hard as a rock.

"Right," she muttered.

Then she looked at the horse. "Why don't we eat that?" she demanded. "It's dead anyway."

Nakor knelt down in front of her. Keeping his voice low, he explained "I don't like to kill other animals, as you may have noticed. Normally, though, I'd be more than willing to let you butcher the horse."

He glanced back at Whoo and Pynne. "But pixies have an overwhelming sense of disgust at those who eat the flesh of other creatures. To them, it's the same as cannibalism. To watch you eat that horse would be as repulsive to them as it would be for you to watch someone eat your child."

Jenn nodded.

"We have enough food for the next day or two," Nakor added. "Once we eat that, we can start to worry."

Galadrion was slicing the straps on the saddle with a sharp dagger. "This way nobody will be able to use what we leave behind," she explained, tossing the now-useless saddle into the woods.

After that, they turned and began walking toward the cliff. Seeing them leaving, Flame flew from his perch and landed gracefully on Nakor's shoulder.

The next hour passed uneventfully. At one point, a squirrel hissed menacingly at the travelers from a tree. A loud shriek from Flame was enough to send it dashing away, leaping from branch to branch.

> I kind of wish I'd written an Evil Squirrel fight.

Nakor grinned and ruffled Flame's neck feathers. Shortly after that, Galadrion gestured for a halt. Her hearing was superior to even Nakor's, and she had detected a faint noise up ahead.

"There's something up there," she said quietly. The pixies vanished immediately.

As they walked, the trees began to thin. Nakor began to faintly make out the murmur of voices in the distance.

Cautiously, they moved forward. Minutes later, they halted again. They were standing in back of a large, canvas tent. In front of them, the forest opened up into an enormous clearing. Hundreds of tents and crude huts were scattered randomly around the area. Toward the center of the clearing, more permanent structures of wood and stone could be seen.

> Don't you hate when you're walking through the woods, and suddenly, BAM! You're in a tent!

"I don't remember this being here," Nakor whispered.

"Olara's city?" Jenn asked, remembering Pynne's report.

"I guess."

He pointed at the far edge of the clearing. A huge cliff, sunk into the mountain, stretched hundreds of feet into the sky. It looked as if something had taken an enormous bite out of the mountain in front of them.

"The temple entrance is at the base of that cliff," Nakor said.

"That's in full view of this city!" Pynne hissed in protest. "Whoo and I could get to it, but what are the rest of you going to do?"

Nakor thought quietly to himself. "First let's go around the city and get as close to the cliff as we can," he suggested. "If we wait for nightfall, it should be easier to sneak inside."

He looked at the others, hoping someone had a better idea. Nobody spoke.

With an internal sigh, Nakor backed away from the clearing and began the long walk around it. Nobody spoke as they followed behind.

CHAPTER SEVEN

D ARKNESS FELL.

> Darkness jumped back to its feet and quickly
> looked around to see if anyone had noticed.

Hundreds of campfires spread a soft orange glow over
the city. The clamoring of Olara's followers had fallen to a
faint murmur as people gradually made their way to their
beds for the night.

> It's basically a big evil summer camp. I skipped
> over the part where everyone sat around roasting
> evil s'mores.

"All the light will make it harder for anyone to see us,"
Jenn whispered. "Their eyes won't be used to the darkness."

> I think I understand what I was trying to say
> there, but reading it hurts my brain.

They crouched together at the base of the cliff, partially hidden by a clump of bare, twisted trees. Several hundred feet ahead, they could see two of Olara's priests standing guard in front of the temple entrance.

"Any idea on how we get past them?" Nakor asked, jerking a thumb at the guards.

"Wait until they get tired," Whoo suggested. "Then sneak up and knock them out."

"Dangerous," Galadrion commented. "If anyone notices us, we'll be trapped out in the open."

"I'd love to hear a better plan," Whoo said. He looked around, but nobody said anything.

"I'm getting sick of all this waiting," Jenn grumbled to herself. Nakor grinned and shifted position, making himself more comfortable.

An hour went by. The moon crawled slowly across the sky, until it was directly overhead. As the moon neared the peak of its journey, the dim light shining down from above began to increase, adding to the illumination provided by the few remaining campfires.

> The moon is directly overhead, and *nearing* the
> peak of its journey? The celestial mechanics of
> this world are fascinating.

One of the guards sat with his back against the cliff. His head hung limply, chin resting against his chest. He was clearly asleep.

His companion leaned against the rock wall, arms crossed. He yawned, but seemed unwilling to succumb to sleep.

It was contagious. Nakor, watching closely, fought hard to stifle an enormous yawn.

"You know," Jenn observed, "if we wait any longer, that

moon's gonna light up the entire cliffside."

Nakor looked up. She was right, any attempt to sneak into the temple would have to be now, when the guards were weary and the night was still dark enough to conceal them. He stood up.

Gesturing silently, Nakor began to move carefully in the direction of the temple. He hugged his cloak around himself, using the dark material to blend into the shadows. Galadrion and Jenn followed behind.

Soon, they were within fifty feet of the temple. The guards had still not noticed. Nakor stopped and turned to Galadrion.

"How do you want to do this?" he asked, keeping his voice low. "If they have the chance to shout, it's over."

Galadrion glanced over at the guards. "What about that sleep spell you did with Whoo?"

Nakor shook his head. "I'd have to be touching them. And even if I could get that close, the spell still takes a few seconds to work. It would give them all the time they needed to sound the alarm."

"I think we're going to have to kill them," Galadrion said.

Nakor nodded. "I don't like it, but I don't see any other way to get in unseen."

"You realize that they'll come after us once they find the bodies?" Jenn asked.

Nakor's reply was drowned out by a loud scream. He tensed, momentarily fearing that their presence had been discovered. Any trace of weariness vanished from his features.

> Suddenly, a convenient distraction arrived!

The sleeping guard leapt to his feet, wiping drool from the corner of his mouth with one hand. He swung his arms back and forth once, loosening the muscles.

> Someone's screaming! Time to leap into action...just as soon as I do some warm-up exercises and stretches.

"That came from inside the temple!" Galadrion hissed.

"I know," Nakor answered.

Up ahead, a woman ran out of the temple entrance. One of the guards stepped forward and caught her by the arm, pivoting on one foot to swing her to the ground. She started to get up, only to find the other man holding a dagger to her throat. She collapsed into a heap, sobbing.

"Wouldn't it be easier to just tie them up to begin with?" asked the guard who still gripped to the girl's arm tightly in his hand.

"Yeah," commented the other, sheathing his dagger. "But Olara likes it when they try to escape. She likes to play games with them, getting their hopes up and all that."

> Because she's EVIL!

"Come on, get up," said the first, nudging the crying woman with his foot. She looked about sixteen years old, with matted brown hair that came down to the middle of her back. She was dressed in a dirty white dress that did little to conceal her thinness.

"That girl looks like she hasn't eaten in a week," Pynne whispered, outraged.

The two men dragged the weeping girl to her feet and began walking toward the center of the camp, leaving the temple unguarded.

"Let's go," Nakor said quietly.

> Thank you for your help, random sixteen-year-old girl! We'd try to save you, but we have Important Quest Stuff to do. Plus we already have one teenage girl in the party, so our quota's full!

Sorry.

Moving swiftly, they made their way to the temple entrance. It consisted of a dark crack in the cliffside, barely big enough for a grown man to fit through. A faint light could be seen from within.

"Go," Nakor said, waving the others on. A slight fluttering of wings told him Whoo and Pynne had landed and were walking inside. Jenn followed behind.

Galadrion was ducking down to enter when they heard the scream. She looked back.

From the temple, there was a clear view to the center of the city. They could see the back of the girl, arms stretched out and tied between two trees. She was struggling madly to escape, nearly dislocating her shoulders in her efforts to yank her wrists free.

"Nakor," Galadrion began.

"I see it," he answered. In front of the girl, Olara stood dressed in a shimmering black robe. All around her, priests watched silently as she slowly drew her dagger. The girl stopped struggling and moaned in terror.

"What's going on?" came Jenn's voice from within the temple.

Nakor looked at Galadrion. His face was a stone mask, hiding whatever he was feeling.

"Inside."

Galadrion looked over at the girl, who stared in horror at the advancing goddess. "Don't be afraid," Olara said with a smile, "it will all be over soon."

"Now!" Nakor hissed. Galadrion stared at him. The mask was gone, replaced by an expression of helpless fury.

Yes, a nameless teenager is being killed, but the *real* focus is Nakor's angsty elf-pain!

I wanna be the angstiest,
Like no one ever was!

> *So much elf-pain, throughout the quest,*
> *To wallow is my cause!*
>
> Um…yeah, that probably only made sense to those of you familiar with the Pokemon theme.

The priests started to chant rhythmically in the distance. Galadrion nodded slowly and ducked inside. Nakor followed, closing his eyes as he heard the screaming begin again.

They were in a small tunnel, barely tall enough for Nakor or Galadrion to stand in. Nobody said anything about the muffled screams from outside.

"This should open up into a large room up ahead," Nakor whispered. "That's where the light is coming from."

The tunnel twisted and turned, causing Pynne and Whoo to bump their wings more than once. Flame cooed softly from Nakor's shoulder, disliking the cramped tunnel.

Then they came around another bend in the tunnel and saw a room before them. It was large and roughly octagonal, with doors in each of the eight walls. A black obsidian altar stood in the middle of the room. To either side of the altar was a small white pillar, supporting a crystalline statue of a spider. Torches were mounted on the walls between each of the doors.

Jenn looked up. High above them, enormous stalactites loomed like knives, ready to pierce any who entered. She swallowed hard.

"Most of the doors lead to the lower levels of the temple," Nakor said. "That's where we had to go to find the gems, two years ago. It was down there that I fell through the trap door."

"Do you remember which door?" Jenn asked.

Nakor grinned sheepishly. "Most of the tunnels below are interconnected. But I don't remember which doors lead to the tunnels."

"Then we do this the hard way," Whoo commented.

Nakor felt the pixie move past him in the darkness, walking into the room. Taking a deep breath, he followed.

Once they were all inside, they stopped.

"Any guesses?" Pynne asked.

Jenn started to say something, then paused to look curiously at the two pixies. "Why aren't you invisible?" she asked.

Pynne blinked. She looked over at Whoo, who stared back in amazement. "Uh oh," he said.

"You said magic doesn't work in the temple?" Pynne asked.

Nakor nodded.

Whoo muttered something incomprehensible under his breath.

They all stopped as one of the doors opened. A large man walked into the room, whistling softly to himself. He was dressed in black trousers and a leather weapons harness across his burly chest. At his belt hung a ring of keys. He stopped abruptly and stared at the intruders.

Nobody moved. Then Nakor smiled hesitantly. "Hi," he said.

The man reached over his shoulder and drew out an enormous broadsword. Then, before anyone could react, he stepped forward and plunged the blade down into the altar. Nakor blinked in confusion.

> "Don't mind me. I'm just here for the nightly altar-stabbing."

Whoo and Pynne looked at each other. Then, with a shrug, Whoo pulled his bow off his shoulder and fired in one smooth motion.

> Oh, sure. Let that girl die, but you'll fight to protect the altar?

The arrow pierced the center of the leather harness, sending the man stumbling back into the door.

"Show off," Pynne commented. Then Galadrion vaulted over the altar and used a dagger to finish the man off.

Whoo flew over to join her, studying the man. Bending down, he retrieved the keys from the man's belt.

"Why do we always have to keep killing everyone?" Nakor asked sadly.

> I literally started giggling when I read this line. Oh, Nakor. You poor, magnificently murderous angst-machine.

Whoo looked at him curiously. "I didn't see much of a choice."

> "Didn't you see the way he attacked that innocent, helpless altar?"

"I know," Nakor answered. "I just wish there were a way to avoid it."

"He would have tried to kill us if he had been a little more quick-witted," Galadrion commented. "Maybe he would have tried to stab us instead of that altar."

She looked closely at the surface of the altar, from which the hilt of a broadsword still protruded. "It looks like there was already a crack here for him to stick the sword into," she observed.

Jenn ran over to study the altar. "I wonder what it does," she murmured to herself.

Then Flame let out a loud shriek, flapping his wings while clutching to Nakor's shoulder. He looked down in confusion, trying to figure out what had frightened the bird. He cleared his throat, and the others looked at him expectantly.

"Those pillars didn't used to be empty," he said.

Where two crystal spiders had been, the tops of the

pillars were now bare. They followed Nakor's gaze to where the two spiders sat staring at them from the far side of the room.

> The spiders are very sportsmanlike, and would never attack an opponent who wasn't ready.

As they watched, one spider moved with surprising speed at Nakor. Whipping out his rapier, he leapt to one side and lashed out. There was a metallic clash, and the spider turned to stare menacingly at him. It made a quiet tinkling noise as it began to circle around him.

> Combat tip: always tinkle *before* the fight starts.

"Watch out!" shouted Whoo.

Jenn leapt up onto the altar as the second spider came racing toward her. Whoo fired an arrow at it, but the spider didn't notice.

Pynne flew into the air and began to gesture with her hands. Then she stopped, remembering the uselessness of magic inside the temple. She hovered, feeling helpless, as Whoo fired another futile shot at the spider.

> That's right, magic doesn't work in here. Which means these are perfectly mundane giant crystal spiders, just like the ones you'd find in your back yard.

The spider at the altar stared for a moment. Then it cautiously began to scale the side, climbing after Jenn.

Jenn backed away, then made a running leap off the top of the altar, nimbly avoiding the protruding sword.

The spider dropped down and began to go after Jenn.

Struck by an idea, Pynne flew over and wrenched the sword from its resting place. There was a slight click as it came free, and she looked hopefully over to the spiders.

There was no change. Frustrated, she dropped the sword with a clatter.

Nakor lashed out with his rapier again, driving the spider back with the force of his swing. It glared, its clear eyes reflecting Nakor's image back at him. Then, its pincers spread open and a small stream of clear liquid shot out at Nakor's legs.

> I wrote about a battle with crystal spiders in a short story called "Mightier than the Sword." In the story, the spiders had escaped from a book described as "typical fantasy crap, with goblins and dragons and elves and magic," written by a "third-rate hack." I swear to LeGuin, I wasn't thinking of this book when I wrote that story. At least not consciously.

He looked down in shock as the liquid hardened, encasing his lower legs in the same clear crystal that the spider seemed to be made of. Unable to walk, he swung his sword back and forth, trying to keep the spider at bay.

The spider circled around behind him, evading Nakor's swings. Then it approached, pincers chiming as they opened and closed.

Nakor turned as much as he could, unable to reach the spider with his sword. He watched as it came closer. Then a large object came crashing down, and the spider shattered into pieces.

He looked over at Galadrion, then down at the spider. He grinned. Galadrion had taken one of the heavy pillars and smashed it into the spider. Then Nakor raised an eyebrow. Galadrion was dressed in her customary white shirt and brown trousers. Where was her cloak?

> Galadrion SMASH! Also, this is raised eyebrow count: 14

The second spider thrashed angrily, confused by the black cloth that blinded it.

Quickly, Jenn grabbed at the corners of Galadrion's cloak, pulling them together into a crude sack.

Galadrion walked over and took the trapped spider from Jenn. She whirled it over her head a few times, then sent both the cloak and spider hurling into a wall. There was a crashing sound, and splinters of crystal fell from within the cloak.

Nakor winced as he hammered at his glasslike prison with the hilt of his dagger. Shards of crystal were falling away, and one had sliced a finger. Wrapping his hand with the edge of his robe, he continued to smash his way free.

"We don't seem to be very good at remaining subtle," Whoo observed.

With a strong jerk, Nakor wrenched one of his legs free. He grinned. "I guess we know what the sword did now, don't we?" Reaching down, he freed his other leg. "So, do you think they know we're here?" he asked.

"We weren't exactly quiet," Pynne observed wearily.

There was a shout from the tunnel behind them.

"How dare you intrude upon this sacred site?" demanded a priest of Olara, stepping into the light. He raised a hand. "The price for such insolence is death."

> "Wait," cried Nakor. "We have a coupon for half-price insolence!"

Then he shouted as Flame dove out of the air, clawing at his eyes. He ducked aside and the bird raked one of his cheeks with his talons.

Furious, the priest sent a bolt of green energy crackling at Flame, who dodged nimbly out of the way.

"I thought magic didn't work in here," Jenn shouted.

Nakor concentrated and tried to cast a spell.

"It doesn't," he said, wincing as the pain coursed through his veins. "I guess Olara's priests aren't playing by the rules."

"Oh well," Whoo commented, "I guess it's good that we have non-magical means at our disposal." Then he sent an arrow toward the priest.

> Presumably by shooting it from his bow, but you never know with this crew.

It crumbled into ashes in mid-air. "You seek to defy me in the temple of my mistress?" the priest asked in a menacing voice. Then he sent another bolt of energy toward Whoo.

Instantly, Galadrion shoved the pixie out of the way. The spell caught her in the leg, sending her crashing to the ground clutching her thigh. "Get out of here," she said through clenched teeth.

Pynne grabbed Jenn's hand and flew to the nearest door. "We have to stay," Jenn cried out.

"I can't use my magic, and your dagger isn't going to help," Pynne answered angrily.

They both looked behind, where the priest was advancing on Nakor. Then Pynne opened the door and shoved Jenn from behind. Reluctantly, they moved into the darkness.

> No! Never split the party. It causes such headaches for the poor dungeon master.

Nakor backed away slowly, keeping his rapier up. Behind the priest, Whoo continued to fire arrow after arrow. Like the first, these burned to ashes before getting close to their target. The priest gestured, and Nakor's rapier flew from his hand to land behind him.

Grabbing the altar, Galadrion pulled herself to her feet. Her leg was beginning to heal itself. Limping, she approached the priest from behind.

"I am not so easy to surprise," the priest said. With an

evil grin, he turned and pointed a finger at Galadrion. That was when Nakor rammed his shoulder into the priest's stomach, sending them crashing to the floor.

There was a loud boom, and Nakor was hurled backward. He slid across the stone floor, landing against the wall. Whoo flew over to land next to him.

"You okay?" asked the pixie.

> Okay? He was just flung onto a stone floor hard enough to slide into a wall! He's probably got a concussion, and he'll be lucky if nothing's broken from —

Nakor watched as Galadrion grabbed the priest and lifted him off the ground. Then he looked to the far side of the room, where Pynne and Jenn had escaped.

"Go!" Galadrion yelled. Then she fell back as the priest sent another bolt of energy into her body.

With an angry glare, Nakor wrenched the door open and went through. Whoo followed, pausing to send one last arrow at the priest.

> Oh. Never mind. I guess he's fine.

Galadrion smiled from the floor as they shut the door behind them. Then she looked up at the priest, who towered over her.

She closed her eyes, feeling her wounds begin to regenerate. There were advantages to being a vampire, she thought to herself.

> Like the great dental plan! Wait, I already used that joke, didn't I?

Breathing heavily from his exertions, the priest pulled a dagger from within his cloak. "Your friends will not escape," he said. "They will never leave this temple alive."

Then he smiled and knelt down next to Galadrion. "I'm sorry about this, I really am. But you shouldn't have come here." He grabbed her by the hair and wrenched her head back. Making a clucking noise with his tongue, he brought the knife to Galadrion's throat.

CHAPTER EIGHT

JENN AND PYNNE GLANCED BEHIND, HEARING THE thunderous noise behind them as the priest worked his magic. It was too dark in the tunnel to actually see anything, but they looked anyway. Then they turned and continued down the tunnel.

"So now what do we do?" Jenn asked grumpily.

Pynne didn't know what to say. Ever since she had realized her magic was useless, she had felt vulnerable. Her inability to become invisible made it even worse.

"I guess we try to find that scroll," she said at last.

There was silence, then, as they both felt their way through the damp, cold passage. Soon, even the sounds of fighting had faded from behind them.

"Do you think they're okay?" asked Jenn nervously.

Pynne closed her eyes. "If they were smart, Nakor and Whoo might have escaped through another door."

Jenn didn't say anything. She had seen the priest's magic send Galadrion crashing to the ground. It was very possible that she was dead.

> Or, you know, deader.

"We might have been able to do something," she said angrily.

"Yes," Pynne replied, "we could have died."

Jenn didn't answer.

The tunnel twisted and turned around on itself, with no apparent plan.

> Much like the plot.

"I think we're getting higher, not lower," Pynne observed after a while. Their eyes had adjusted to the darkness by now. A fungus on the walls gave off a faint green glow, enabling them to see.

> Where would the fantasy genre be without convenient glowing fungus to light all those dark dungeon tunnels?

"That's not where we want to be going, right?" Jenn asked.

"Right," Pynne answered with a frown. "Nakor said they were underneath the main temple when he fell through the trap door."

"Great," Jenn muttered to herself.

"Maybe you should have stayed in that city after all," Pynne teased.

Jenn grunted in reply.

Up ahead, the tunnel branched off in two directions. Picking one at random, they marched down the left tunnel.

Soon the tunnels split off again, then another time. Shortly after that, they had become confused and hopelessly lost.

"I think we've been here before," Pynne commented.

Frustrated, Jenn looked around. The tunnel went in four different directions, not including the way they had just come from. "Which way did we go last time?" she asked.

Pynne pointed at the third tunnel.

"Fine," Jenn said, "Then let's take a different one." Then she turned and began marching up the rightmost tunnel. With a shrug, Pynne followed.

Unlike the others, this corridor seemed relatively straight. As they walked on, it began to get warmer as well.

Jenn stopped abruptly.

"What is it?" asked Pynne.

"This isn't right," Jenn answered. She didn't know exactly what it was, but something about this tunnel seemed wrong somehow. "It's too uniform, it doesn't match the other tunnels," she commented.

Then she knelt down on the ground. "And look, there's about an inch of dust down here," she observed.

Pynne, whose wings had been dragging in the dust for the past ten minutes, only nodded. "Nobody's been this way for a long time," she said.

"I don't like it," Jenn said.

"Do you want to go back?" Pynne asked.

Jenn considered for a moment. But the idea of spending another half hour backtracking was incredibly distasteful. "No," she answered, "I just don't like it, that's all."

Pynne nodded sympathetically.

After a while, they began to notice a pale light coming from in front of them. It grew brighter as they moved on. It was also becoming warmer. Jenn had begun to sweat, and Pynne was gently fanning herself with her wings.

"Look," Pynne said with a wry grin, "there's a light at the end of the tunnel."

Jenn groaned, but it was true. Up ahead, a bright red light filled their vision. In reality, it was little more than a pale glow. But after all the time spent in near-total darkness, it was almost blinding.

As they walked closer, the cause of the light became clear. The tunnel stopped abruptly, opening into emptiness.

Jenn and Pynne crept up to the very edge of the tunnel and looked out.

They were on one side of an enormous cavern, hundreds of feet from the opposite side. Jenn gasped involuntarily as she looked down.

Far below, a fiery red river of lava flowed across the cavern floor, vanishing into one of the walls. "All this is inside the mountain?" Jenn asked, awestruck.

> I'm beginning to question the geological consistency of this environment.

"I've never seen anything like it," Pynne answered.

They stared for a moment, just looking out at the immense emptiness that stretched before them.

"Well, now we know why it's so hot," Jenn commented.

Pynne frowned. "What's that on the far side?" she asked, pointing.

> Talking cow? (Which probably only makes sense to people who are old enough to remember *The Far Side*.)

Jenn squinted. "I don't see anything."

"Stay here," Pynne said. Then she leapt out into the air, flying toward the other side.

"What am I going to do?" Jenn asked, rolling her eyes, "follow you?"

She peered out over the edge, waiting for Pynne to return. The cavern walls seemed to drop straight down forever, coming to an abrupt stop when they met the river of lava. Jenn blinked and shook her head as a brief wave of dizziness passed over her. Pulling her head back into the tunnel, she sat against a wall and waited.

Pynne returned soon, landing gracefully in front of Jenn. She wiped the sweat from her forehead.

"There's a passageway on the far side of the cavern,

too," she said. "I suspect that there was once a bridge between the two tunnels."

Jenn nodded. "That's nice, but I don't see how it's of any use. I can't exactly fly across, you know."

Ignoring the sarcasm, Pynne continued. "I also saw something else on the way back. There's a ledge built into the wall a couple of feet below us."

"Where does it go?" Jenn asked.

"Down," Pynne answered. "Then there's a door that probably leads back into more tunnels."

"I couldn't see it when I looked out," Jenn protested.

"I know. It looked as if it were designed to be hidden from anyone on this side of the cavern."

"Well," Jenn said thoughtfully, "we need to get deeper underground, right?"

Pynne nodded. "But I'm not strong enough to fly you down," she added.

"Damn," Jenn muttered to herself. Then she peered out over the edge again. She was still unable to see the ledge Pynne was speaking of, but this time she saw something else.

"Look at this, there are holes on the cavern wall." On either side of the opening, two large holes had been dug into the rock. "Hold my hand," Jenn said, stretching farther out.

Pynne grabbed the hand and leaned back, using her weight to keep Jenn from falling. "You know," she said, "it might be a good idea for me to be the one checking this out. Unless you've suddenly sprouted wings?"

Ignoring her, Jenn studied the holes for a moment. On impulse, she stuck her hand into one. Then she allowed Pynne to pull her back into the tunnel.

"It's only one hole," she said. "It curves around on itself on the inside."

I've read this scene three times, trying to visualize what they're looking at. I failed. I'm sure I

> had it all figured out in my head at the time, though.

"That's probably where they would have anchored the bridge," Pynne guessed. "Whoever 'they' were."

"Who cares?" asked Jenn. She untied the rope belt at her waist and leaned out again. Threading one end of it through the hole, she tied a quick knot. "Will that get me down to the ledge?" she asked.

The rope stretched a good two feet below the floor of the tunnel. Pynne nodded slowly.

"Then let's go!" Jenn said excitedly. Grabbing the rope in one hand, she carefully sat down, dangling her feet over the edge. Then, closing her eyes, she allowed herself to slip out of the tunnel.

Pynne launched herself into the cavern and turned to help steady Jenn.

Lowering herself down, Jenn kicked out at empty air. That must be where the ledge is at, she thought to herself. Then she looked down.

Pynne saw the color drain from her face. Grasping her gently by the waist, Pynne whispered reassuringly. "You're not going to fall. Just lower yourself a little more, then jump onto the ledge."

"Jump?" Jenn hissed, eyes wide. She had no fear of heights, but looking down into the lava below frightened her. The thought passed through her mind that the only thing preventing her from falling was her flimsy rope belt. Her arms were beginning to tire.

"Would you rather climb back up?" Pynne asked, worried.

"I can't!" Jenn answered. The fear in her voice was clear.

> "I can't! Mostly because the plot says so!"

"Jenn," Pynne began in a calm voice, "take your left

hand and put it at the bottom of the rope."

Wordlessly, she obeyed.

"Now put your right hand just above your left."

Jenn did so, cursing quietly as she reached the knotted end of the rope belt.

> Now put your left hand in, and then you shake it all about.

"Okay," Pynne said reassuringly, "now when I count to three, let go."

"What?" Jenn cried. She could see the ledge now, but there was no way for her to get to it. She could try to swing back and forth, but she didn't know if her rope was strong enough. "Let go?" she demanded.

"I'm going to push you onto the ledge," Pynne explained.

"I don't like this," Jenn moaned, closing her eyes.

> Writing tip: There's absolutely nothing wrong with using "said" for dialogue instead of constantly reaching for other words. Though Sir Arthur Conan Doyle liked to use "ejaculated," for a dialogue tag, and he's done pretty well with those Sherlock Holmes stories, so what do I know?

"Would you rather just hang there?" Pynne asked. "You'd get awfully hungry after a while." She studied Jenn's situation. "Not to mention that you look rather silly."

Jenn glared angrily at the pixie.

"It's your choice," Pynne offered.

"Count to three!" Jenn hissed. "And if you let me fall, I swear my spirit will haunt you for the rest of your life!"

Pynne grinned. "One."

Jenn closed her eyes and prayed.

"Two."

She held her breath.

"Three."

Jenn let go, feeling her stomach clench as she started to fall. Then there was a violent shove on her back, and she crashed onto the ledge. She stayed there for a minute, breathing rapidly and unwilling to move.

A moment later, Pynne landed beside her, holding her belt. "You did it," she said.

Jenn sat up slowly. "We better not have to come back this way," she said between gasps.

After giving Jenn a few minutes to recover, they began walking along the ledge. It looked as if someone had scraped an enormous groove into the cavern wall. The groove was about three feet wide and five feet high, and had a remarkably flat floor. It slanted downward at a steep angle, and there were occasional steps carved into the rock to ease their descent.

Jenn swore as she scraper the top of her head against the rock above. She looked at Pynne, who walked along quite comfortably in the short tunnel.

"Great," Jenn muttered, "a pixie tunnel."

"What was that?" Pynne asked, glancing back.

"Nothing."

"I think we'll turn back into the tunnels pretty soon," Pynne said.

They stopped as the ledge ended abruptly. To the right, built into the rock, was a large wooden door.

"The hinges aren't even rusted," Jenn said in amazement.

"You need moisture to make rust," Pynne commented, blotting the sweat on her forehead with a sleeve. She moved to open the door.

"It's locked," Pynne said in disgust.

Jenn grinned. "Out of the way, pixie," she said, reaching inside her shirt.

Pynne stepped off of the ledge, hovering a few feet away.

Producing a pair of thin metal wires, Jenn knelt down in front of the door. A moment later, she stood back up. With a flourish, she opened it.

"It's unlocked now."

Rolling her eyes, Pynne began to walk down the tunnel. Still grinning, Jenn followed behind.

Up ahead, the short figure stood motionlessly. About four feet tall, the figure rested his hands on the hilt of a large axe, allowing the head of the weapon to rest on the floor. He hadn't moved for the past ten minutes that Jenn and Pynne had been watching.

They looked at each other, confused. In the dim light given off by the green fungus and the fading glow of the lava, it was difficult to see clearly.

"I say we go talk to him," Pynne whispered.

Jenn turned to argue, then grinned.

"I can't see you."

Pynne could see Jenn without difficulty. "That means my magic is working again," she said with a smile. "Stay here."

> "...it was difficult to see clearly." A few lines later: "Pynne could see Jenn without difficulty." This was my attempt to metaphorically demonstrate that the characters inhabit an everchanging and inconsistent world...or it would have been, if I had ever bothered to develop the world.

Jenn sat impatiently, waiting. Moments later, she heard Pynne's laughter.

"It's okay," she called.

Standing up, Jenn walked toward Pynne, now visible, who stood contemplating the figure guarding the door.

"He's a dwarf," Pynne said as she walked up.

It was indeed. And from the looks of it, he had been dead

for a long time. The skin was dried and shrunken, where the moisture had been leeched from the body. Long, curly hair still protruded from under a pointed helm, matching the scraggly beard that dangled over the chest. Further detail was obscured by a thick layer of dust that covered the figure.

> This is what Pynne was laughing about? Pixies think dead bodies are freaking hilarious!

Suddenly it all made sense. "These must be dwarven tunnels," Jenn said. It would explain the short, cramped passageways she had been complaining about.

Pynne nodded, still studying the dwarf. "He died here, guarding the door. There's nothing around to indicate why."

Jenn's brow wrinkled. "What could have killed him so suddenly?" she asked.

> He had to read the first draft of this book. Poor fellow.

"I don't know."

They turned to study the door before them. Unlike the last door they had encountered, this one was carved entirely from stone. The only exception was the metal lock built into one side.

"Private folks, weren't they," Pynne commented. "Care to open this one as well?"

Jenn's lockpicks reappeared in her hands again, as if by magic. She peered into the keyhole, then frowned. Her cautious, professional side took over.

In order to be a thief, one had to be patient, careful, and a little bit reckless. This is what she had been taught for years. You never knew what you would have to do in order to pull off a successful job. Sometimes you had to trust a hunch.

"This isn't right," she said, turning to the dead dwarf. Her repugnance at the corpse vanished as she took a large, prominent key from his belt.

Pynne coughed as Jenn blew dust from the cast iron key. Then she began to wipe it on her sleeve, polishing away the last of the dust.

"No rust," she commented. Then she peered at it closely. "No scratches, either."

Pynne looked at her curiously.

"No scrapes from sliding across the metal of the lock. No marks from being used." She dropped the key on the floor.

"That key has never been used to open this or any other door," Jenn said. Then she began looking around the edge of the door, peering at the walls, the floor, and the ceiling.

"So what is it for?" Pynne asked.

Without looking up, Jenn began to explain. "Someone didn't want people to get to this room. That's why it was so hard to get to the ledge outside."

She got down on her hands and knees, still looking around intently. "If, by chance, someone gets onto the ledge and past the first door, the guard here kills them or something."

"But if you want to be really clever," she said, looking up at Pynne, "you add another guard."

She pointed at a tiny set of holes to one side of the door. "Then when the intruder kills the dwarf, steals the key, and tries to open the door..."

"They die," Pynne finished. She peered at the small holes. "Darts?" she asked.

"Probably poisoned, if someone knew what they were doing," Jenn said with a nod.

"So how do we open it?"

Jenn knelt back down and slid one hand underneath the crack of the door. She grimaced as the rough stone scraped the skin from her knuckles. Then there was a click.

With a look of triumph, Jenn stood up and pushed on the door. It swung open quite easily, a tribute to the stone-working abilities of its makers.

Together they walked into the small room beyond. Then they stopped, stunned by what lay before them.

The room was about ten feet square. A stone shelf stood about two feet off the ground, carved out of the same rock as the rest of the walls.

"I guess this is why they had the guard," Jenn whispered.

The shelf was full of gold and silver. Thousands of round coins were neatly stacked in one corner of the room. In another, rectangular bars of gold were piled in a criss-crossing pattern. Underneath the shelf sat several small wooden chests.

> Oh look, we've found Scrooge McDuck's money bin!

Pynne wandered over to one side to study a pile of round, uncut gems. Casually, she picked up a ruby as big around as her thumb. "No dust in here," she noted.

"Maybe they had some sort of magical way to protect this stuff from the elements," Jenn guessed.

"Or else the door kept anything from blowing in," Pynne said.

Jenn walked over to a small rack of weapons. Selecting an intricately designed dagger, she peered closely at it. The wire-wrapped hilt still shone in the faint light. The blade was made of a mottled silver metal Jenn didn't recognize.

"Dwarven steel," Pynne commented, looking over at the dagger.

"What?"

Pynne pointed at the dagger. "Dwarves are masters at working with stone or metal," she explained. "One of the things dwarves are famous for is their ability to forge weapons that are stronger and hold an edge better than any that aren't dwarf-made."

"That little knife there is probably worth enough to feed a small town for a month."

Try as she might, Jenn couldn't keep a smile from spreading across her face. "A month?" she asked. She grabbed the leather sheath that had been placed unobtrusively behind the weapons rack. Slipping the dagger and sheath into her belt, she turned to study the room.

Overwhelmed for the moment, she walked over to study a small, leather-bound book that lay unobtrusively in one corner.

"What's it say?" Pynne asked.

"How am I supposed to know?" Jenn demanded. "I don't speak dwarven."

Pynne wandered over and gently took the book out of her hands to study.

"This isn't dwarven," she said as a frown spread across her face. "It's elvish."

Out of habit, she turned to the last page. It was blank. She flipped backward through the pages until she came to one with writing on it. Then her eyes widened.

"What is it?" Jenn asked.

"It's a journal," Pynne answered, still staring at the book. "Averlon's journal." She began to read.

> You think some of the writing has been stilted before? You ain't seen nothing yet!

I write this, my final entry, as I sit here among the riches of the dwarves. The poor fellow who used to guard this room still stands outside, mummified by the heat of the molten rock below. If my suspicions are correct, he has stood guard there for three thousand years, ever since Olara was cast into her astral prison.

My studies have revealed that Olara is a thief of life itself. She drains the soul in order to grow in power. I fear that in the battle between Olara and the other gods, she may have taken the life of all that used to live beneath this mountain. The Book of the Spider, which I so foolishly destroyed in my fright, indicates that this massive death will become all too common if Olara's resurrection is successful.

That Olara's resurrection is inevitable I have no doubt. She is imprisoned, helpless, for the time being. But I have talked to her priests. Even now, they work at finding a way to free her from that prison, and I have no doubt that they will someday succeed.

> Dun, dun, DUN!

To that end, I have created Olatha-shyre. I have spent weeks wandering these ancient tunnels, struggling as I tried to create my spell. It is a work of the greater magic, that art which transcends the narrow definition of magic as we know it. It is an art lost thousands of years ago, preserved only in the vaults of our temples.

> Ah, the lost arts. So ancient and mysterious and ancient. Like the Sloth style of Kung Fu, or the Tantric Hokey-Pokey.

It is also an art which none have practiced in centuries. I have been forced to create a spell using skills which none today can teach. But finally, I believe I have succeeded.

Olatha-shyre, the Spider's Bane, is a masterpiece of subtlety. Its power lies in its simplicity. But I will write no more. Only yesterday, one of her priests tracked me down, seeking to destroy the scroll upon which I wrote my spell. It is for that reason that I have hidden Olatha-shyre within these dwarven tunnels.

Today I leave, to begin my journey home. I fear I shall not live to see my friends again. The priests know that I entered their sacred temple, and they will be waiting for me when I leave. But I must devote all of my energies to re-

turning home, for I must be sure that the knowledge of Olatha-shyre is not lost.

—Averlon Lan'thar

> PS, If I don't make it, please delete my browser history.

Carefully, Pynne shut the book. "Thomas said that he made it to the temple, but died shortly after he got there."

Jenn nodded without saying anything, overwhelmed by the incredible sense of age coming from the room around her.

"All of this has been here for thousands of years," she whispered.

"Obviously Olara's priests never found this room," Pynne commented. "I wonder how Averlon discovered it."

"Probably read about these tunnels back in his temple vaults." Jenn looked around the room. "So now what?"

"Averlon said he hid the scroll somewhere in these tunnels," Pynne said, "so I guess we keep looking."

"Well, I'm not going back the way we came."

Pynne grinned. "Like I said, dwarves are masters at working with stone. They could have built an easier way in and out of this room, then hidden it from view somehow."

It took them about a half hour to find it. Jenn, opening one of the chests, noticed a round protrusion of stone from underneath the shelf. After examining it closely, she reached out and tugged on the small knob.

> All right, get your mind out of the gutter.

A two foot square portion of the wall opened into the room, bumping against the chest. Grunting, Jenn and Pynne shoved the heavy chest to one side, allowing the door to swing completely open. They peered through the small portal.

"Grab what you want to take, and let's go," Pynne said, squeezing through the opening.

Jenn looked back, studying the riches that lay before her. "Aren't you taking anything?"

"Too heavy to fly with," Pynne commented. Then she winked. "Besides, we can always come back."

With a grin, Jenn followed her through the small doorway. then a thought struck her. "What about Averlon's journal?"

> The thief leaves without taking any of the gold or jewels? That's about as in character as Mister Rogers busting a beer bottle and starting a bar brawl.

Pynne's voice took on a more somber note. "I think it would be safest here, don't you?"

The book had remained safely hidden from Olara for two thousand years in that room. Jenn nodded slowly, and pulled the door shut behind her.

As the door shut, the light from the lava flow was lost. Once again they were plunged into blackness.

Out of curiosity, Jenn knelt down and felt for the outlines of the small door. There was no trace of anything unusual.

"It probably can't even be opened from this side," Pynne commented, hearing the sounds of Jenn's search. "If we want to get back in, we'll have to do it the hard way."

She smiled, hearing Jenn's groans. "Shall we keep looking?" Pynne asked.

Jenn stood and placed one hand on the damp stone of the wall. Using that hand as a guide, she began walking down the tunnel, ducking to keep from bumping her head.

"I guess we shall," Pynne muttered to herself, hearing Jenn leave.

CHAPTER NINE

NAKOR AND WHOO RAN SILENTLY THROUGH THE tunnels. There was a faint light from ahead, giving off enough illumination to see where they were going.

"Darkhesh," Nakor cursed, feeling the empty scabbard bounce against his hip.

"What was that?" Whoo asked.

"A dwarvish word Scrunchy once tried to teach me," Nakor said. "It means 'cheesecake.'"

"Cheesecake?"

Nakor grinned. "I never got the pronunciation quite right. It was rather frustrating for him."

> This was an actual thing in our D&D game.

Whoo laughed, thinking of the legendary impatience of dwarven warriors. Then he came to an abrupt halt.

"Look up there," he whispered.

Up ahead, the tunnel widened out. There were torches on one wall, and several doors on the other. Sitting casually on the floor, a guard sat honing a dagger. He was dressed in the same style of black trousers and weapons harness as the man they had encountered earlier.

> Can we all pause a moment to appreciate the artistry of that sentence? "Sitting casually on the floor, a guard sat..." That's freaking art right there! Someone nominate this thing for the Hugo Award already!

From behind one of the doors, a weak voice cried out.

The man glanced up. With a snarl, he hurled his dagger at the door where it embedded itself in the brown wood, quivering slightly. There was silence.

"Kill him?" Whoo asked quietly.

Nakor shook his head. "Not this time." He stood up. Without looking back, he whispered "Cover me."

Whoo raised an eyebrow. Then he crouched down and pulled an arrow out of his nearly empty quiver.

> Raised eyebrow count: 15

The guard leapt to his feet as Nakor approached. Drawing a large broadsword, he pointed it at Nakor's chest.

"Who are you and what are you doing here?" he demanded.

Nakor stopped a few feet away from the man. "I need your keys," he said quietly.

> Anyone else imagining Nakor trying to do the Jedi mind trick here?

The guard looked confused for a moment. This wasn't how people were supposed to react with a sword pointed at them. "If I had the keys, I'd be locking you up with the rest of them," he said, nodding at the wooden doors. "But I don't. Anton took them when he went on break."

Then he grinned. "So I guess I have to just kill you now."

There was the ring of metal on metal, and then the guard was staring dumbly at his sword, now lying several feet behind him.

> Wait, WTF just happened?

Whoo stepped into view, holding another arrow nocked and ready. "You talk too much," he chided.

> Aha! I think we're supposed to believe Whoo used one of his little pixie arrows to shoot a broadsword out of a man's hand. Totally plausible!

Then he turned to Nakor. "Courtesy of Anton, I assume," he said, handing him the keys he had taken from the guard earlier.

Nakor nodded his thanks, then looked back at the guard. Reaching over, he removed a pair of daggers from the man's harness.

Then he turned and began unlocking the doors, one at a time. The guard looked as if he were going to protest, but Whoo raised an eyebrow and he thought better of it.

> Raised eyebrow count: 16

Soon, a group of eleven people had been freed. Several were small children, and all of them looked weak and hungry. One man, the largest, stepped forward and studied the helpless guard.

"Are we to die now?" he asked. Several of the prisoners put their arms around the children protectively.

Nakor shook his head sadly. "I hope not," he answered. "All I can do right now is give you a choice." He handed the man the ring of keys, followed by the two daggers he had taken from the guard. Another man picked up the sword, and a small boy wrenched the knife free of the door.

Then Nakor looked at the guard and gestured at one of the empty cells behind him. Looking at the angry prisoners, he added "It's probably safer."

The guard eyed the men who looked thoughtfully at their new weapons and swallowed hard. Moving swiftly, he stepped into the room and pulled the door shut behind.

"If you would?" Nakor said to the man with the keys.

"Robert," he said as he locked the door. "Robert DeBaer."

Nakor quickly introduced himself and Whoo. "Well Robert," he said, "all of you have a decision to make."

He turned to look at the former prisoners. "We can lead you out of the temple, but it would be leading you straight to Olara and her followers."

Robert and the others conferred quietly. Then Robert turned to address Nakor and Whoo.

"We're not staying here," he said in a determined voice. "Show us the way out."

Nakor nodded. Spinning around on one heel, he began walking back down the corridor. He stopped to take a torch off the wall as he walked.

"Are you going with us?" Robert asked as they walked. He seemed to have been the spokesperson for the group.

"No," Nakor said. "We aren't finished in here yet." There was a quiet determination in his voice.

"What about the children?" Nakor asked, lowering his voice.

> I feel like there was supposed to be something between Nakor's two paragraphs there. Right now, it reads like a glitch in the Matrix.

Robert lowered his head slightly, and suddenly Nakor knew what he was about to say.

"They murdered my son the second night we were

here."

Bitterness and grief were plain upon his face, but only a slight quiver betrayed those emotions in his voice.

"He was one of three prisoners executed as an object lesson. One of us had resisted a guard the day before." His knuckles were white where he clenched the guard's sword. "Olara brought us out to watch as they were tortured to death."

> I'm starting to think I was a very bleak and depressed college student.

"I've talked with the others while the children slept," he continued. "Freeing the few children who still live is all we want anymore."

Glancing back to assure himself nobody could overhear, he continued. "If that fails, we will kill them ourselves. They will not be allowed torture any of these children."

They came to the large door at the end of the tunnel. Nakor gestured for silence and passed his torch back to one of the prisoners. Nakor stepped close to Robert, moving so he could whisper into his ear.

"There may be a priest in that room beyond."

Robert nodded to show he understood.

"If so," Nakor continued, "we wait until he leaves." He looked sadly at Whoo. "He may already have killed one of the people we came in with."

Taking a deep breath, Nakor opened the door a crack and peered out. Then, sighing in relief, he opened it the rest of the way and stepped into the room.

A grin spread over his face. Looking at the dead priest, he glanced back at Robert.

"Then again, he may not have."

The body lay sprawled against the altar, arms and legs jutting from the body at random angles. His dagger still lay on the ground where it had fallen. The priest's back had clearly been broken when he landed.

"What kind of friends do you have?" Robert asked in-credulously.

Studying the knife on the ground, Nakor glanced back at him. "She doesn't like knives."

From among the huddled group of prisoners one of the women whispered in amazement.

"She?"

Nakor grinned. Then he bent over and handed the dagger to Robert. Pointing at the small crack between two of the walls, he spoke.

"That tunnel will lead you out of the temple." He walked over to retrieve his rapier from where it had fallen earlier.

Robert turned to one of the women. "Lenora," he said, handing the dagger to her. They looked each other in the eye for a moment, but said nothing.

Stepping away, Lenora tucked the knife inside her belt. Robert turned to Nakor.

"The children will not be taken," he repeated in a quiet voice.

Nakor and Whoo watched in silence as Robert led the prisoners down the tunnel.

"Good luck," Whoo whispered.

"You know," Whoo commented as they walked down the tunnel, "You don't act like other elves I've met."

Nakor smiled. They were exploring another tunnel at random, guided by the torch he had taken from behind the altar.

"Why not?" Nakor asked.

"I don't know exactly." Whoo frowned, thinking. "You're more expressive, more open somehow."

"Most elves are more withdrawn?" Nakor suggested.

"Yes," Whoo said. "No offense, but you act more like a human than an elf."

"Good guess."

He was quiet for a minute, trying to figure out what to say next. "I only spent the first two years of my life living with other elves."

Whoo listened in silence as Nakor talked.

"You know that elves live in the woods," Nakor began. "They take very good care of those woods, protecting the trees and the land they live in. Unfortunately, they can't protect it from everything."

> You know this because you're familiar with the *Big Book of Fantasy Clichés*, from which this entire novel is derived.

"The forest where I was born burned to the ground when I was two. A human town nearby needed the land, so the Duke ordered the forest cleared. Some of the people had heard rumors of the elven village living there, but they didn't care."

> Thus was my elf-pain born!

"For some reason, my parents had taken me out of the forest that day. They might have been collecting food, or perhaps they were investigating the odd gathering of humans at the forest's edge."

> But more likely it was just another random plot contrivance.

"I don't know exactly what happened. I suspect they saw the fire, and ran back to help. To keep me safe, they left me hidden under a bush."

Nakor shrugged. "I was found nearly a day later, contentedly throwing rocks into a stream. The humans who found me decided to adopt me as their own son."

"That was nice of them," Whoo commented. "They

could have just left you to die."

Nakor closed his eyes, remembering.

"You motherless elven bastard!" his father screamed.

Nakor cowered back against the wall, holding the small, dead rabbit in front of him as a shield. His father grabbed it away from him.

"I told you I wanted quail for supper!"

"It's the cold, sir," Nakor said weakly, "it's driven the animals away." Then he fell as his father backhanded him across the face.

"Don't give me any of your excuses." He gestured at a longbow that hung on a wall behind him. "If you'd learn to use a real weapon rather than that piddly-ass sling you carry, maybe you could start and earn your keep around here."

The bow had been found among the burned remains of the elven village. Two days after the forest was destroyed, a party of humans had explored the village, looking for souvenirs. There had been little regret over the massive deaths of the elves. The general response had been to blame the destruction on the Duke who had ordered the forest cleared.

Nakor had never had any desire to use the bow. For him, it was a tangible reminder of what he had lost.

"Give me that," his father yelled, grabbing Nakor's sling. Then he whipped it against Nakor's arm.

Nakor winced, glancing at the pink welt above his elbow.

"Get out there and chop some firewood, you useless little bastard," his father cried, giving him another slap with the sling.

"Yes sir," Nakor whispered, racing out the door.

Nakor turned to Whoo with an ironic half-smile. "Yeah, it was really nice of them."

I don't even know what to say at this point. I'm

out of snark. Feel free to make up your own.

He had later learned that the human town in which he had lived was started as an experiment. It was a place for the nearby Duke to dump the less desirable elements of society. Nakor had grown up surrounded by criminals, those people whose crimes weren't serious to warrant death, but who could not be allowed to live with 'civilized' people.

"So when did you leave?" Whoo asked.

"I was probably about nineteen."

It had been seventeen years since Nakor had been found. Having overslept that morning, he had been unable to finish preparing breakfast before his parents had woken up.

"Where's our food?" his father screamed.

Nakor's mother sat quietly, as she always did when her husband's temper flared. "I'm almost done," Nakor cried out, scrambling to set the bacon on the plates.

In his haste, Nakor dropped one of the plates, scattering food at his father's feet.

"You bloody jackass!" his father screamed. Tipping his chair over backward, he stormed out of the room.

Nakor got down and began cleaning up the mess. A moment later, he felt something smash across his back. There was a loud snap, and a moment later something was dropped onto the floor next to him.

Turning his head, he saw the elven bow his father had hit him with. It had broken with the impact, and now lay uselessly next to him.

Gently, he reached out and touched the bow. The only link to his true family now lay ruined beside him. An intense anger began to spread through his veins.

"You useless little elf," his father shouted. "Get off the floor and get your lazy ass back there to cook my breakfast!"

Moving slowly, Nakor stood. His back hurt terribly, but the pain was brushed aside by the rage inside him.

Interpreting Nakor's sluggishness as an insult, his father hit him.

Nakor was close to his adult height. Years of intense physical labor had strengthened his body, although that strength was difficult to see on his wiry elven form.

He touched his lip, then looked slowly at the blood on his finger.

"That's right," Nakor hissed, "I'm an elf." He looked down at the food on the floor. "Cook your own bloody breakfast."

His father's eyes widened.

This time, Nakor was prepared for the blow. Catching his father's arm, Nakor threw him into the table. His mother screamed.

"How dare..." his father's voice trailed off as Nakor brought a kitchen knife to his throat.

"If you ever touch me again," Nakor whispered, "I will kill you. Is that clear?"

Fear shone in his father's eyes, and he nodded desperately.

Turning, Nakor walked toward the door. He listened to the sound of his father getting up off the table. He continued walking, listening to the gentle footfalls behind him. When they got close enough, Nakor spun and punched his father in the stomach.

"Funny," Nakor commented as his father gasped for breath, "A human wouldn't have heard you." He studied the knife in his hand.

"I guess we're lucky I'm an elf."

In disgust, he flipped the knife at his father's feet. It stuck in the wooden floor, vibrating slightly.

Whistling to himself, Nakor walked out of the house.

> I like to imagine he was humming "I Will Survive" as he left. Or maybe something by Pat Benatar.

Nakor shrugged as he and Whoo walked down the tunnel. "I guess I just needed my space."

Whoo was about to say something else when the floor disappeared beneath them. Reflexively, Whoo flapped his wings and shot up several feet. Flame launched himself from Nakor's shoulders and hovered next to Whoo.

Bending his knees to absorb some of the impact, Nakor crashed onto the ground ten feet below. He stood up, then winced. In his efforts to keep from falling on the lit torch, he had scraped his elbow on the hard stone floor.

He looked up at Whoo and Flame, who were both peering down in curiosity. With a whistle, he summoned the bird to his wrist. Using beak and talon, Flame climbed up the sleeve of Nakor's shirt to rest on his shoulder. Whoo floated gracefully down to join them.

"I don't want to hear one word about footerlings," Nakor said as they looked around.

Whoo grinned. After a respectful pause, he asked "That was the trap door you were talking about?"

"Yes. If I hadn't been so lost in thought, I would have recognized the tunnel."

"Well," Whoo began, "Maybe you should try not to think so much."

Nakor didn't bother to respond. Closing his eyes, he tried to remember which way to go.

After a moment, he opened his eyes. Without speaking, he raised the torch and began walking down the tunnel.

"Are you sure this is the right way?" Whoo asked.

"Nope."

Shaking his head, Whoo followed.

A large rat raced into the middle of the hall. There it stood on its hind legs and stared curiously at the pair.

Stopping, they watched the rat for a moment. It didn't seem to have any fear of man.

"Do you think Olara could be using animals to spy on us?" Whoo speculated.

Nakor raised an eyebrow. With a shrug, he placed his index finger in front of Flame. In one swift motion, he swung his finger and pointed at the rat.

Raised eyebrow count: 17

Shrieking loudly, Flame launched himself at the small rodent.

It never had a chance. Dropping down to all fours, the rat spun and raced back to the wall. Flame scooped him up in one claw, then flapped his wings and landed on the ground.

Nakor began to walk down the hall once more.

"What about Flame?" Whoo asked.

"He'll be along as soon as he's done eating," Nakor said.

Whoo nodded. Animals killed other animals for food, this was the natural order of things. It was the planned, deliberate killing of animals by sentient beings that he despised. Still, he couldn't quite repress a shudder of revulsion as he glanced back to see Flame happily eating the dead rat.

"You could have tried to talk to it," Whoo commented.

"Whether it was a spy or not, that rat had been living here for a while," Nakor answered. "That means it would have been affected by whatever changed that deer we saw earlier."

"Besides, Flame hasn't eaten in a while," Nakor added. He didn't think Whoo's theory was correct. True, it was within Olara's power to use animals to spy on the group, but it wasn't her style. Nakor had a much more unpleasant suspicion about that matter.

"So which way?" asked Whoo, breaking Nakor's train of thought.

He looked up. The tunnel branched off in two directions in front of them. It was a familiar sight.

"Back the way we came," said Nakor, smiling.

"I knew you were going to say that," Whoo muttered.

"That's where I was when the skeletons attacked," Nakor explained. "I had to turn and run back the other way."

They passed Flame, who glanced up from preening himself as they walked by. Seemingly unconcerned, the fire falcon reached over and smoothed out one last uncooperative feather. Then, as the pair were beginning to pass out of sight, Flame leapt into the air and flew back to his perch on Nakor's shoulder.

> Wait, back in chapter two, I said Flame was an owl. I'm so confused!

A few minutes later, Nakor stopped again.

"This is where I waited with my sling," he muttered. "Then I got wounded in the legs. I crawled away..."

He looked up. "I felt a breeze on my face."

Passing the torch to Whoo, Nakor knelt down and began crawling down the tunnel. Amused, Whoo leaned against a wall and watched.

Soon, Nakor grinned and leapt to his feet. Reaching out, he shoved a part of the tunnel wall. There was a click, and a portion of the wall slid backward a few inches. With a shove, Nakor opened the door.

"After you," he said, gesturing to Whoo.

Holding the torch high, Whoo walked into the small room. Nakor followed, grinning.

Once inside, Nakor turned and shoved the door shut.

"You're sure this is the right room?" Whoo asked.

As an answer, Nakor rolled up his sleeve to show the scratches on his elbow. He gestured, and the cuts closed.

"I'm sure," Nakor said, brushing the dried blood off his skin.

He pointed at the door on the opposite wall. "I never opened it, so I don't know where we're going from now on."

"Then we're even," Whoo replied, opening the door. He glanced worriedly at the torch. "Nakor, we're about to run out of light."

With a smile, Nakor took the torch from Whoo's hand. Blowing hard, he extinguished the last of the dim flames. Then he concentrated, and a small ball of fire appeared in one hand.

Tossing the useless torch aside, Nakor walked through the door.

"Show off," Whoo muttered, walking behind.

CHAPTER TEN

IT WASN'T LONG BEFORE THEY CAME TO ANOTHER door. Nakor opened it, then leapt back in surprise.

A large vicious-looking dragon was coiled around a white pedestal. On top of the pedestal sat an ivory spider, clutching a crystal sphere.

The dragon growled. Polished green scales gleamed, reflecting the light of Nakor's flame.

> With this dragon, I believe we've won Fantasy Cliché BINGO!

"Now what?" Nakor whispered, looking over at Whoo.

Whoo grinned. "I'll handle this," he commented, winking at Nakor. Then he marched boldly into the room, nocking an arrow. "I say we kill it," he said in a loud voice.

"What?" demanded an outraged voice. The dragon shimmered briefly, then vanished.

"You wouldn't dare!" Pynne shouted, running over to embrace the pixie. Jenn looked happily at Nakor and

Whoo.

"We heard you at the door," Jenn explained, "So Pynne cast the dragon illusion over us. How did you know?"

Whoo grinned, then turned to Pynne.

"You always make your illusions with such big, black eyes," he chastised. "Dragons have yellow eyes."

> Pynne does everything anime style.

Pynne rolled her own blue eyes. "Like most people are going to stop and study the eyes."

"I did." Whoo said, still grinning.

Jenn's smile vanished. "What about Galadrion?"

"We found the priest," Nakor said. "He was very dead, and Galadrion was gone."

Jenn relaxed. "So she's alive."

"Nakor," Pynne said excitedly, "We found Averlon's journal."

His eyes widened. "Do you have it here? Did it have the scroll? Did it explain what we have to do?"

Pynne smiled at the jumble of questions pouring from Nakor's mouth. "No, no, and no," she answered. "We didn't want to take the risk of Olara getting a hold of it."

"What about the scroll?" Whoo asked.

"Averlon hid it somewhere in these tunnels," Jenn butted in.

"Just like Nakor and I guessed," she added with an obnoxious smile.

> I am really tired of this author's habit of splitting dialogue by one character and breaking it into two paragraphs for no reason. It's confusing and obnoxious. What's wrong with this guy? Hasn't he ever read a book to see how dialogue is supposed to work?

"We just came straight from the lower levels of the

temple," Whoo said. "So the scroll must be hidden some-where ahead."

Pynne frowned. "We've explored everything behind us, and it's not there. There wasn't much to explore, really. A few empty rooms, nothing more."

> Random lava. Ancient treasure vault. You know, the usual.

"Oh no," Jenn groaned, "You don't suppose it's on the other side of the canyon, do you?"

"Canyon?" Nakor asked, raising an eyebrow.

> Raised eyebrow count: 18

"The dwarves used to have a bridge leading to more tunnels," Pynne explained. "But from what I saw, it hasn't been there in a long time."

"Dwarves?" Whoo asked.

"Yeah," Jenn answered. "Didn't you know these were dwarven tunnels?"

Whoo looked at Nakor, who shrugged.

"I don't want to go back," Jenn said.

Nakor turned to study the sculpture on the pedestal. "This wasn't part of your illusion, then?" he asked Pynne.

"No, that was here when we walked in."

"Have you had a chance to study it?" Nakor asked.

"We only got here a few minutes before you did," Jenn answered.

He peered at the sphere, held tightly within the spider's legs. It was highly polished, reflecting the light he held in his hand. There was a slight blue tinge to the crystal. He raised his eyes, noticing that the spider seemed to be watching him.

"Averlon would have wanted us to be able to find the scroll," Nakor said quietly.

"But he needed to keep it safe from Olara," Pynne pointed out, "So he couldn't have made it easy to find."

Nakor closed his eyes and cast a quick spell. Opening them again, he smiled at the green glow of magic that permeated the sphere.

"Let's find out how easy it is," Nakor whispered. Reaching out, he touched the sphere with one hand. Nothing happened.

With a frown, he extinguished the flame in his hand, plunging the room into darkness. He touched the crystal with his other hand. Still, there was no response.

"What exactly are you trying to do?" Pynne asked curiously.

Nakor frowned. He had assumed that this magical artifact must have something to do with finding Olatha-Shyre. Wrinkling his brow in concentration, he recreated his small flame, lighting the room. Then he turned to answer Pynne.

"Watch out!" Jenn cried out.

Behind him, the statue of the spider had begun moving. Nakor ducked, and it leapt over his head and skidded across the floor.

> What a shocking twist that no one could have anticipated, despite the exact same thing having happened earlier in the book!

"Can't Olara do anything better than create living statues?" Pynne asked as she flew up out of reach.

"Goddess or not, she's still a footerling," Whoo answered. Drawing one of his last arrows, he fired at the spider.

Whoo's eyes widened as it passed through the statue without harming it. "Uh oh," he muttered.

The spider turned and looked at Nakor. With a shrug, Nakor tossed his flame at the small stone creature. Like Whoo's arrow, it passed through without harm.

Annoyed by the disturbance, Flame flapped over to perch upon the now unguarded crystal.

"I don't know what this thing is," Pynne said, "But it's no

illusion. I'd know."

Nakor drew his rapier and began to advance.

Without warning, the spider leapt high into the air. Nakor lashed out, but was too slow. It crashed into Pynne's hovering form, sending them both crashing to the ground.

Pynne screamed as the spider's pincers closed on her neck. Then she was still.

"Pynne!" Whoo cried out. Instantly, he fired both of his remaining arrows at the spider, to no effect.

The spider turned slowly, studying the opponents who remained. Then, as if it had come to a decision, it began to advance upon Jenn.

She backed away, holding her dwarven dagger in front of her. She sensed Nakor coming up next to her, sword ready.

Nakor was still in shock. He glanced over at Pynne's still form. She wasn't breathing. A wave of grief threatened to overcome him, but he brushed it away for the moment. He couldn't afford to break his concentration.

True story: When I was writing this book, I would let my girlfriend read what I had written at the end of each day. She seemed to really like it. Then again, she was dating me, so we know she had questionable taste.

When she read this scene where Pynne dies, she got so mad she broke up with me...which probably says something about the health of our relationship. (We did end up getting back together a little while later.) But hey, if the point of writing is to evoke emotion, then I certainly succeeded!

This is one of the reasons I no longer let anyone read my first drafts.

Faster than any natural creature could move, the spider

leapt again. Jenn screamed and brought her dagger up, hoping to fend off the creature.

Without thinking, Nakor crashed into her, shoving her out of the way. He tried to swing his rapier at the spider, but was too late. It landed on his chest, sending him stumbling back.

Panicking, he clawed at the spider as it prepared to bite. His hands passed through it with no effect, and Nakor watched in horror as the pincers tore through his shirt and pierced his chest.

He felt pain spreading through his body. Stumbling to his knees, Nakor tried desperately to heal himself, to purge his body of the poison racing through his veins. Then everything faded to blackness.

Nakor was in a large, empty room. Everything was white. The floor was covered in white tile, as was the ceiling. The walls seemed to be made of some sort of polished white rock, and pure white pillars formed a perfect circle around Nakor. The overall feeling was one of emptiness.

> "The character wakes up in an empty, feature-less, white room." Translation: the author couldn't be bothered to do any description.

Confused, he looked down at his chest. The shirt was undamaged, giving no evidence of the spider's bite.

"Hello?" he called out, looking around.

His voice echoed around him. Then, slowly, a figure began to materialize in front of him.

Nakor didn't move. He just watched in silence the man, dressed in grey robes, stepped forward. He was tall, probably an inch past six feet. His long hair was pure grey, and his face displayed the lines of age. Graceful pointed ears displayed his elven heritage, as did the pure green eyes that stared intently at Nakor.

> You can tell this guy is very important because he has green eyes.

For a long time, neither spoke. Nakor began to get the impression that the elf would be perfectly content to stand in silence for the rest of eternity, if need be.

Eventually, Nakor broke the silence. "Where are we?"

The elf frowned. "That's a difficult thing to explain."

His voice was clear and strong, showing no signs of age. "I guess you could say that we aren't anywhere."

Nakor raised an eyebrow.

> Raised eyebrow count: 19

"Who are you?" the elf asked.

"My name is Nakor. And you are?"

"I am the caretaker of this place. My name is Averlon."

"You're Averlon?" Nakor asked incredulously.

"Not precisely," he elf answered with a faint smile. "But I was created in his image. Averlon made me, a long time ago, and left me here to wait." He shrugged. "I have no other name, and the true Averlon no longer has need of it."

"What are you waiting for?"

"Perhaps I've been waiting for you, Nakor," Averlon answered. "You have passed the first test, and are obviously no priest of Olara."

A dark frown spread across Nakor's features. "Test?"

"Had you been such a priest, your reaction to the spider would have been quite different. You would have gladly laid down your life and allowed it to kill you, if that was its desire."

> Wait, you mean all we have to do to fight these evil priests is dump a bucket of black widows on them?

"In addition," he continued, "by sacrificing your life to

save your young friend, you proved your loyalty."

"Pynne is dead," Nakor said bluntly. "Your test killed her."

> Nakor completely misses the implications of that "sacrificing your life" bit here.

Averlon glanced down momentarily. "Surely you understand the necessity of preventing Olatha-Shyre from falling into the wrong hands. I am sorry if your friend was harmed, but perhaps we will be able to do something to rectify that situation."

"Such as?" Nakor demanded. He was too angry and hurt over Pynne's death to worry about being civil.

"All must be done at its proper time," Averlon said softly. "First you must prove to me that you are the one who should receive Olatha-Shyre."

"How do I do that?"

"You can't," Averlon answered with a smile. "This is the other problem I face. There is nothing you could do to prove yourself that could not be faked by one with evil in his heart."

He looked into Nakor's eyes. It was a disconcerting look, but it was somehow familiar as well. Then Nakor remembered. It was the same look that Thomas had given him back in his small monastery.

"Therefore," Averlon continued, "we must rely on what you have already done."

Nakor said nothing as Averlon reached out to gently rest his first two fingers upon Nakor's temple. There was a momentary flash of pain.

"Do not be alarmed," came Averlon's soothing voice. It was muffled somehow, as if Nakor was hearing it from a great distance. "This will not harm you."

> Mostly because you're already dead.

Suddenly images began racing through Nakor's mind. Scenes from his life were remembered in an instant, then vanished again. He saw himself hitting his human father, then a moment later he was hurling a sling bullet at a skeleton. He saw Whoo and Pynne, eating happily at his table. He saw Galadrion, walking alone in the street as she had been the first time Nakor had met her.

> I use the word "suddenly" 37 times in this manuscript. I'd have to re-read to be certain, but I suspect that's 37 times more than I needed.

Then he began to see scenes from his original exploration of the temple. He remembered in astonishing detail what had happened the night that he had helped to free Olara. He watched again as she casually stabbed one of her priests.

In an instant, he remembered meeting friends, and watching them die. He saw all of the mistakes he had ever made displayed before him. The image of every person he had ever been forced to kill flashed through his mind.

Then it was over. Averlon drew back his hand, and Nakor collapsed onto his knees. Tears were racing down his face. For a moment, neither spoke.

After taking a moment to regain his composure, Nakor looked up. "You saw?" he asked.

Averlon nodded. "I saw what I needed to see." He rested a hand gently on the side of Nakor's face. "You have endured much pain, and much anger."

> So. Much. Elf-pain.

Nakor closed his eyes and didn't respond.

"You still have much to learn, Morelain," Averlon said.

"Morelain?" Nakor asked, looking up.

"It is the name given to you by your true parents, Nakor. It was there, buried in your memory where you could not find it."

"But if I can't remember it," Nakor began.

"I could not afford to be limited by what you can and can not remember," Averlon explained. "I had to know everything. Only then could I be sure."

> Tip for writers: "can not" is not the same as "cannot."

He studied Nakor for a moment. "Go in peace, Nakor Morelain."

Nakor blinked, finding himself in darkness. He was standing before the crystal, grasping it with both hands.

"What exactly are you trying to do?" Pynne asked curiously.

He pulled away from the crystal, wincing at the stiffness in his arms. He paused for a moment, focussing the energy needed to create the small flame in his left hand.

Seeing Pynne standing curiously before him, Nakor smiled.

> Yay! It was all just a dream, and Pynne's still alive! That wasn't a cheap or overused writer trick *at all*.

"Are you okay?" Whoo asked.

For an answer, Nakor simply held up the scroll in his right hand.

They sat around waiting while Nakor studied the spell. There was no evidence of his ever having been gone. The statue of the spider still stood atop the crystal. Whoo still had three unused arrows in his quiver.

Upon asking, Nakor had discovered that no time had elapsed while he endured Averlon's trial. The others had been shocked to hear Nakor's description of what had occurred. Pynne, especially, had seemed rather disconcerted by the description of her death.

"So what does it do?" Jenn demanded impatiently.

Nakor looked up from the scroll. "I don't know," he answered, a puzzled look on his face. "It's a very simple spell, but it doesn't look like it does anything."

"In his journal, Averlon said it was a masterpiece of subtlety," Pynne commented.

Nakor looked back down at the scroll. "It's beyond my understanding," he commented. A few minutes later, he sighed and stood up.

"Are you ready to go?" Nakor asked.

"Shouldn't you study that some more?" Pynne asked.

Wordlessly, Nakor turned the scroll so that she could see it. Only four lines of writing spanned the top part of the page. The rest was taken up by an elaborate drawing of a spider sitting upon a jewelled throne.

"I memorized it," Nakor said.

"Four lines?" Pynne demanded incredulously. Even the simplest of spells took up most of a page when written down. It was not possible to put a spell on paper in so brief a space.

Nakor shrugged. Rolling up the scroll, he tucked it into his backpack.

"Don't worry," he said with a grin, "It will either work or it won't."

Pynne groaned softly.

A more somber mood slowly settled over the group as they turned and began to make their way back out of the temple.

As they passed out of the dwarven tunnels, Nakor suddenly cried out in pain and grabbed his hand. The flame went out, and they were in darkness once more.

"Ouch," Nakor whispered.

"What happened?" Jenn demanded.

"My magic stopped working when we passed through

that door," he answered. "I burnt my hand."

Whoo laughed quietly as he pulled the secret door shut behind them. "Next time just grab an extra torch."

Together, Whoo and Nakor led them back down the corridors, to where the trap door still hung open above them. The faint glow given off by the fungus on the walls allowed them to make their way without incident.

Once there, Whoo and Pynne flew up, carrying the rope Nakor had brought. Then they lowered one end and leaned back, bracing themselves as well as they could.

Jenn went first, as she was lighter than Nakor. The pixies flapped their wings, struggling to support her weight. Whoo gave a sigh of relief as she grabbed one edge of the hole and pulled herself through.

There was a loud flutter of wings, and Flame emerged. He hopped away from the others and peered curiously down at Nakor.

With Jenn helping, Nakor was able to climb up through the trap door. Then he recoiled his rope and replaced it in his backpack.

"Let's go find Galadrion and get out of here," Nakor said, walking back toward the octagonal room where they had last seen her. "She must have taken a different tunnel," he mused. "But eventually she'll have to come back to that room. We can hide and wait for her there."

"What if another of those priests find us?" Jenn asked.

Nakor glanced at her. "We'll just have to hide really well."

As it turned out, they didn't have to hide at all. Galadrion was waiting for them when they entered the room. She wasn't alone.

Her arms were held by two men who stood to either side of her. A little ways away, a black-robed priest motioned for them to come closer.

"Welcome back, Nakor," the priest said in a mocking voice. "We've been waiting for you."

He looked over at Galadrion in confusion. She stared back at him and shook her head slightly.

"Please toss your weapons into a pile," the priest continued.

Still watching Galadrion, Nakor slowly drew his rapier. He looked back at the priest, remembering the earlier fight in this room. Galadrion's clothing still had burn marks from that fight. Wordlessly, he dropped the rapier on the ground.

Soon, Whoo's bow joined it, followed by Jenn's newly acquired dagger. Within moments, a small pile of weapons lay on the floor before them.

The priest raised an eyebrow and pointed at Jenn. With an angry glare, she reached inside her shirt and tossed her other dagger into the pile.

Raised eyebrow count: 20

"Thank you," the priest said. Then he snapped his fingers, as if suddenly remembering something.

"Oh yes," he said, "I'll need Olatha-shyre as well, if you don't mind."

Nakor looked at him curiously. "Olatha-shyre?"

"If you wish to play games, we can," the priest said. "However, the consequences will not be pleasant." He pointed a finger, and a beam of energy shot into the wall above Jenn's head. She jumped aside and looked back, seeing a scorched black mark where the beam had hit the stone.

"I have a finger-laser! *Pew, pew, pew!*"

Nakor nodded slowly. He slid his pack off his shoulders and reached inside.

"Nakor," Pynne hissed.

He looked sadly at her. "I know."

Then he took the scroll from the pack showed it to the

priest. With a laugh, the priest sent another bolt of energy at the scroll. It crumbled into ashes.

> If I was a bad guy, I'd want to make sure I was actually destroying the real scroll, as opposed to, say, an old scrap of elven pornography Nakor picked up in the woods or something. But what do I know?

Nakor cried out, grabbing his hand. Whoo and Pynne looked at each other in despair.

"Now," the priest said with a smile, "You will come with me."

As they were led out of the temple, Nakor looked back at Galadrion. He wondered how they had captured her, and how these two men were able to hold her prisoner. Then he looked closer, studying them by the light of the torch the priest carried.

Neither of the men were breathing. Galadrion had been captured by a pair of vampires.

CHAPTER ELEVEN

GALADRION HAD SMILED AS NAKOR AND WHOO escaped through one of the doors. She hoped they would be able to find the spell they were looking for. Or perhaps Pynne and Jenn would find it. At least they had gotten away, she thought to herself. Then she turned back to look at the priest who knelt beside her.

"I'm sorry about this, I really am. But you shouldn't have come here." The priest grabbed Galadrion's hair and wrenched her head back. Making a clucking noise with his tongue, he brought the knife up under her chin.

"Maybe you're right," Galadrion said quietly, closing her eyes.

Then he drew the blade across her throat.

The priest's eyes widened, seeing that his knife had no effect. Galadrion reached up and grabbed him by the front of his cloak. Then he was hurled through the air and crashed against the altar. The knife clattered to the ground.

Oh sure, I could have written, "Galadrion hurled

> him through the air." But why use active voice
> for an action scene when I can use passive voice
> and make it 158% less exciting?

"Maybe not."

Wincing, Galadrion got to her feet. Her wounds weren't healing properly, she noted. Looking around, she tried to remember which door Jenn and Pynne had gone through. Picking one, she limped over and grabbed a torch from the wall next to the door. Then she opened the door and began walking down the tunnel.

Almost immediately, she came to a set of poorly carved stairs that circled downward. Where they ended, two different tunnels led off into the darkness.

Galadrion stopped at the bottom of the stairs and peered down the tunnels. There didn't seem to be any difference between the two. With a mental sigh, she began walking down the right tunnel.

She studied the corridor as she walked. It was obviously well-used, for the floor was free of dirt. The walls were covered with some sort of gray-blue fungus that clung tenaciously to the stone.

Cobwebs filled the uneven cracks and spaces in the ceiling. Absently, Galadrion raised her torch up until the flame licked at one of the webs. She watched as the web curled away from the torch, burning into nothingness. A spider fell, landing next to her foot.

> Smokey the Owlbear says, "Only you can pre-
> vent dungeon fires!"

She crushed it with her boot.

"If only it were that easy," she whispered to herself. Then she froze, hearing voices from ahead.

It was too far away to make out what was being said. All she could tell was that they were male voices. Perhaps this tunnel connected to the one Whoo and Nakor escaped through.

Confident in her ability to protect herself, Galadrion raised her torch and began walking toward the voices.

As she got closer, the voices suddenly stopped. Galadrion began to feel a faint buzzing in her mind. It was painless, and familiar for some reason. She stopped and waited.

Soon she could see a light approaching. Two men walked into view. One man held an oil-burning lantern in, while the other had a sword drawn.

> He held an oil-burning lantern in *what?* Don't leave me in suspense. His hand? His mouth? His boxer shorts?

The one carrying the lantern stepped forward to study Galadrion. He was dressed all in black, with a sword strapped to his side. His sleek brown hair was tied into a ponytail, and a neatly trimmed goatee decorated his chin. Deep brown eyes stared past a hooked nose as he contemplated Galadrion.

"We weren't informed of your arrival," he said at last.

Suddenly Galadrion realized why the buzzing in her mind was familiar. It was a sensation she hadn't felt for nearly thirty years.

After being bitten by a vampire, Galadrion had fled from her home. She had dug herself a shelter deep in the forest. There, she was able to escape from the rest of the world, covering the entrance with sticks and leaves. Then, a few weeks later, he had come back.

He had been ready to receive Galadrion's gratitude for the gift he had bestowed on her. Instead, she had tried futilely to kill him, repeatedly stabbing him with her dagger. After a while, she stopped, realizing the hopelessness of it. He had laughed, bowed courteously to her, and departed.

All the while they had been together, Galadrion had felt that same sensation in the back of her mind. She had been too enraged at the time to think anything of it, but now it made sense.

> All the while they were together? They spent what, five minutes together after she was turned?

A feeling of dread came over Galadrion then, as she realized that she faced her own kind. She was still weak from the priest's attack.

The second vampire sheathed his sword and stepped forward. He was slightly taller and more muscular than his companion. His blond hair was tied in a similar ponytail, but he was cleanshaven. Like the other, he was dressed in black. The only exception was a deep blue sash tied around his waist.

> The bad guys all wear black. Because Evil has a dress code. (The Evil Undergarments are the worst.)

"I am Gavin," he said, "this is Derek."

The other vampire nodded.

"I'm Galadrion," she answered.

"Why did Olara send you?" asked Gavin.

Hope filled her heart. They thought she had been sent down here to join them!

"I was sent to look for the intruders," she answered, thinking quickly.

They looked at each other. "Intruders?" Derek asked.

Galadrion cursed silently. She had assumed they were down here looking for her and her companions. Now, it looked like she had just put Nakor and the others in greater danger.

"They found a dead priest up above," Galadrion explained. "Olara wants whoever killed him found and brought to her."

Gavin nodded. "Olara has been paranoid about outsiders

ever since she got a hold of that prophesy."

"Prophesy?" Galadrion inquired politely.

"You haven't heard?" Derek asked.

She shook her head.

"Apparently some old priestess predicted that Olara would be killed by that elf who helped resurrect her," he said. "To make things worse, he disappeared right after she found out."

> Vampires are rather chatty, aren't they?

"So, now she's got us patrolling the tunnels down here, just to be safe," Gavin added. He rolled his eyes. "We've been down here for two straight days."

Galadrion was relieved. It was obvious that these two hadn't heard the rumors about Nakor's vampiress companion. That was probably a result of being alone in the temple for so long.

"Do you think it's him?" Galadrion asked cautiously.

"Nakor," Derek said. "The elf's name is Nakor."

"It takes a lot to kill one of Olara's priests inside the temple," Gavin said with a frown. "From what I've heard, Nakor doesn't have that kind of power. Especially without his magic."

"Maybe he figured out how to get his magic back," Galadrion ventured.

"I doubt it," said Gavin. "Olara has to do a special ceremony for a priest before he can cast spells in here. She only goes to that effort for a few of the exceptionally gifted ones."

"He could have had help," Derek offered.

"Does it really matter who the intruder is?" Galadrion asked, avoiding that topic.

"Galadrion's right," Gavin said, "we should just find whoever it is and take them to Olara."

They began to walk down the tunnel.

"You okay?" Gavin asked, noticing Galadrion's limp.

She snorted in disgust. "I mouthed off to one of those exceptionally gifted priests." She pointed to the scorches on her shirt and trousers. "This is what I got for it."

Derek clapped a hand on her shoulder. "We all get that from time to time. One of these days I'm going to teach some priests what happens when you annoy a vampire."

"Shut your mouth," Gavin said in disgust. "If anyone catches you talking like that, you're going to get burned just like her."

Up ahead, a door was built into the left wall. They stopped there, and Derek took a small key from around his neck to unlock it.

"You new?" he asked Galadrion.

"Yeah," she replied.

"Then you've probably never been in here." She shook her head, and he continued. "This here is where we make our base while we're living in the lower levels."

He swung the door inside and set his lantern on a round wooden table. It was a small, cramped room filled with various weapons, tools, and several barrels.

"Extra oil," Gavin commented, pointing at the barrels.

Galadrion nodded, staring at a large map that on one wall. It was obviously a map of the temple. She could see the octagonal room they had found, with eight tunnels twisting out in different directions.

> I'm sad to say I don't think I have my map of this dungeon anymore. Otherwise, I could have a fancy front-of-the-book map, just like all the real fantasy novels!

The temple was larger than she had expected. Corridors twisted around each other, forming a complex labyrinth. The occasional room broke the maze of tunnels.

"What's this?" she asked, pointing to a tunnel that stopped abruptly at one side of the map.

Derek glanced over. "That one opens up into a huge

cavern. It's a dead end, nobody's been there for years."

"Nice place to end it all, though," Gavin said dryly. "There's a molten river at the bottom of the cavern," he added for Galadrion's benefit.

"How nice," she said, matching his dry tone.

Derek cleared his throat, trying to get people's attention. "Do either of you need anything here?" he asked. "I've already grabbed a few extra flasks of oil."

Gavin looked at Galadrion, who shook her head.

"Then let's go," he said.

They walked out of the room, and Derek locked the door behind them.

"I think we should stick together," Gavin said.

Derek looked at him questioningly.

"Galadrion here doesn't know the tunnels like we do," he explained. "Besides, I'm not too keen on the idea of going up alone against someone who took out one of the black-robes."

Derek laughed. "You afraid of this guy, Gavin?"

"Just being careful," he answered. "Olara thinks this elf has the power to kill her. If so, there's always the chance he'd be able to do something to us, too."

"Whatever," Derek said, walking ahead.

Following behind, Gavin looked over to Galadrion. "Derek's a little on the aggressive side. He can be a little on the stupid side sometimes, too."

"I heard that," Derek called from up ahead.

"Good!" Gavin yelled back. "Now shut up before you warn everybody in the whole bloody temple that we're here."

After that, they walked in silence.

"Why don't we head up to the altar room and see if there's any clues about which passage this intruder took?" Gavin suggested.

"Sure, whatever," Derek said grumpily. He was still sulking about being yelled at earlier.

Galadrion just nodded silently in agreement. She was finding it disturbingly easy to fit in with these people. Since becoming a vampire, Galadrion had tried to avoid people as much as possible. That was why she had been so willing to live with Nakor, isolated in the forest.

Now, for the first time, she was spending time with her own kind. There was none of the hatred, none of the fear she endured from the "mortals," as Gavin and Derek referred to them. She felt as if she belonged. For the first time in over a quarter of a century, she no longer felt like a monster.

Nakor had been the only one who had treated her with anything approaching this type of acceptance. Jenn seemed to like her, but Jenn didn't understand exactly what she was yet. As for Whoo and Pynne, well, perhaps pixies had a different perception of vampires than footerlings.

Her musings were interrupted as they halted before a door. Yanking it open, Derek led them back into the altar room.

"Two of the torches are gone from the wall mounts," Gavin noted immediately.

"I took one of them," Galadrion explained.

"Hey, look at this," Derek called. He was kneeling next to the body of the dead priest, still crumpled against the altar.

"It looks like something just hurled him through the air," Gavin commented, studying the corpse. "And look over here."

He had turned his head and was now examining the shattered remains of one of the crystal spiders. The pillar still lay on top of the pile of splinters, where Galadrion had thrown it.

"The other one's over here," Galadrion called, trying to conceal her nervousness.

"What could do this kind of damage?" Derek asked, surveying the room. "Even I'd be hard pressed to get close enough to do that to a priest," he admitted.

"You might have been right about Nakor finding a way to get his magic back," Gavin speculated, glancing at Galadrion. "If so, he's more powerful than we've been told."

Galadrion breathed a quiet sigh of relief. They didn't suspect anything. Now she just needed to find a way to divert the pair so that the others could escape. Her comfort at being with other vampires had evaporated when she was reminded that these two would kill her friends without hesitation.

She knelt down by Gavin to study the pillar-crushed spider. "I'm impressed," she commented.

"But none of this tells us which way to go," Gavin said, glancing around the room. "Any ideas?"

"How about that one," Galadrion said, pointing to a door she knew was the wrong one.

"Why that one?" Derek asked curiously.

Galadrion shrugged. "I figure your guess is as good as mine." Then she smiled. "But I'd still rather go with mine."

They were turning to re-enter the tunnels when they heard a noise behind them. Spinning, they beheld a priest walking into the room.

"Greetings, Niuris," Gavin said respectfully.

> I have no idea where I came up with that name.
> Or how to pronounce it. But at least there are
> no random apostrophes, eh?

"Gavin," the priest replied absently, nodding his head in greeting. "Who is your friend?"

Gavin frowned. "This is Galadrion, she's new."

Niuris studied her for a moment. Then his eyes widened.

"You fool!" he shouted. "One of Nakor's companions is a female vampire!"

Gavin and Derek both whirled to grab her, but they

were too slow. Galadrion had already leapt forward and pulled the pillar off of the dead spider. Straining, she hurled it at the priest.

Niuris waved his hand, and the pillar crumbled into dust in mid-air. He blinked as the dust blew past him, momentarily blinding him.

Seeing her chance, Galadrion reached over her shoulder to draw her sword. Then she felt a strong hand close across her wrist.

She turned to look into Derek's angry face. A moment later, Gavin grabbed her other arm. She struggled briefly, but it was no use.

"Is it true?" Gavin whispered.

Galadrion looked into his eyes. She felt genuine regret that her brief moment of acceptance was over. Once again, she was the enemy.

"Yes."

"You killed that priest, didn't you?" Derek asked.

She nodded.

Out of Niuris's line of sight, Derek grinned. Leaning closer, he whispered into Galadrion's ear.

"I wish I could have seen it."

"So what do we do with her?" Gavin asked.

"We wait," Niuris answered. "Nakor and his companions are somewhere inside, searching for a spell that will help them against Olara.

"This is the only way out," he said, gesturing at the tunnel behind him. "So we wait here until they return."

They waited for close to an hour, with nobody saying anything. Once or twice Galadrion tested the grips of her captors, but their grasp was like iron. She was trapped.

Then, Nakor led the others into the room. He stopped in surprise, studying the scene before him. Galadrion watched sadly as they were disarmed, and Olatha-shyre was destroyed.

"Now," Niuris said in an arrogant voice, "you will come

with me."

Then he spun on his heel and began walking out of the tunnel. Glancing at the vampires who held Galadrion prisoner, Nakor followed, Jenn and the pixies walking close behind.

"Hey Niuris," Derek yelled, "What time is it outside, anyway?"

"There are still several hours until dawn," the priest called back, "you have nothing to fear."

"Olara is going to be very happy to see you again, Nakor," Niuris continued, turning to look back at his prisoners. "She's been wanting to talk to you for a long time."

"All she had to do was ask," Nakor answered, still holding his wounded hand.

"A goddess does not ask," Niuris said disdainfully, "she commands." He looked over the others as they walked. "Your friends will have to be killed, of course," he said casually.

Nakor tensed. Everyone had been aware of the risks involved, even Jenn. But that didn't make it any easier to deal with, now that they had been captured.

"I don't suppose you'd be willing have an honorable duel for the lives of the prisoners?" Nakor ventured.

Niuris just laughed.

"I didn't think so," Nakor muttered.

> Bad guys are jerks.

Pynne and Whoo glanced at each other. Then they both looked at Jenn.

She was maintaining a facade of nonchalance, but inside Jenn was scared. It was starting to sink in that she was going to die. She kept telling herself that they would escape, somehow, but deep inside her heart a tiny voice was whispering that it was all over. Thirteen years old, and she was going to die.

They were walking out of the temple now, into the moonlit clearing. A little ways away, Olara's city of followers slept. Only the occasional campfire still burned.

> I love that I kept calling this glorified campsite a city.

"You know," Pynne commented, "without Olathashyre, we're really no danger anymore."

"Oh, I know that," Niuris said. "But Olara isn't the kind to forgive and forget." He turned and smiled at Nakor. "Besides, you're family."

"You know," Nakor said, "I think you're forgetting something."

Niuris looked at him disdainfully. "Oh really?"

Nakor nodded vigorously.

"And what might that be?"

He turned and walked up to the two vampires holding Galadrion. Casually, he placed a hand on either of their shoulders. "It has to do with these two gentlemen."

> Bad guys are jerks, but they're so cooperative about patiently waiting while the good guys get ready to do something.

Derek and Gavin both stared at him in confusion.

"So what, precisely, am I forgetting?"

Grinning, Nakor closed his eyes and concentrated. Turning his hands palm up, he conjured two small balls of fire.

"This," he answered.

The vampires' eyes widened. Then Nakor slapped the flames into their faces.

> That's right, Nakor slapped his flaming balls right into...um...never mind.

CHAPTER TWELVE

FORGETTING THEIR PRISONER, DEREK AND GAVIN leapt back, frantically slapping at the flames that began to spread over their hair and clothes. Galadrion leapt forward, trying to avoid the flames.

Nakor took that moment to gesture to Flame. Obeying one of the few commands he recognized, the fire falcon flew off into the night.

"I will kill you myself!" screamed Niuris, raising his hands. Then Jenn punched him in the stomach.

She was too young to do any serious damage, but it was enough to interrupt his spell. Niuris cursed and raised a hand to slap Jenn out of the way.

Whoo dove from above, crashing into Niuris's knees. As he did so, Pynne flew up and kicked him in the throat. They had both been invisible since the moment Nakor cast his spell.

I hope all of this fighting and screaming and burning didn't interrupt anyone's sleep.

Gagging, Niuris fell back to the ground. Grabbing the amulet around his neck, he whispered softly.

"Olara, help your servant."

Derek was no longer moving. Jenn glanced back at his prone form, then looked away in disgust. Death by fire was not a pretty sight, even for a vampire.

Gavin was stumbling around, clutching his face. He had managed to put out the flames, but not before being burned severely. Wounds made by fire were slow to regenerate.

Grabbing him by the shoulders, Galadrion guided Gavin to the ground. "Just stay here," she said quietly, "There's no need for you to be killed too."

Then she walked over to where the others were gathered around Niuris. He had stopped struggling, and now looked up at them with a resigned expression on his face.

"Go on then," he muttered, looking at Galadrion. "Kill me, or drain my blood, just get it over with."

"Yes my dear," came a voice from behind, "kill him."

Olara stood behind them, leaning against the cliffside. She was dressed in the same shimmering black robe she had been wearing earlier. Her raven hair was held back by a delicate silver headpiece.

"It will save me the trouble of executing him for his incompetence," she continued, glaring at Niuris.

Niuris began mumbling incoherently, begging forgiveness. Rolling her eyes, Olara made a gesture of dismissal.

"Go prepare for the ceremony," she said impatiently. "And see if you can handle this without messing up."

Rolling to his feet, Niuris walked swiftly back toward the nearby village.

Olara turned her attention back to the group before her. "Now this is rather unfair," she complained. With a wave of her hand, suddenly Pynne and Whoo were visible once more.

"Much better."

Nakor took a deep breath and began to recite the words to Olatha-shyre. There were only eight words he had to speak. He brought his hand up, palm facing Olara, and focussed all of his energy on casting this spell.

In the middle of his incantation, Nakor felt a sharp blow to the back of his head. He flew to the ground in a heap, and his vision went white for a moment. He blinked, trying to refocus his eyes.

"I'm sorry, Nakor," whispered Galadrion.

He stared at her, in shock. Clutching the back of his head, Nakor tried to sit up. A wave of dizziness overcame him, and he fell back to the ground. "Why?" he asked.

> Because PLOT TWIST!

Nakor could hear Olara laughing, despite the hazy state of his mind.

"Sleep, my friends," Olara said, "for the moment, you must sleep."

The last thing Nakor saw as he lost consciousness was his friends falling to the ground, overcome by Olara's magic.

Jenn looked around the room. There was only one door, locked on the outside. The only window was barred, and too small for anyone to fit through anyway.

She sighed, depressed. Over and over, she watched in her mind as Galadrion stepped forward and struck Nakor in the head. Jenn felt betrayed and miserable. She had come to admire Galadrion, and now she had turned against them.

Jenn looked over to where Galadrion sat quietly in a corner. She and Galadrion were the only two who had recovered from Olara's spell. Ever since waking up, Galadrion had been huddled in the corner, staring at the floor. Peering closer, Jenn saw the faint shine of tears on her cheeks.

Serves her right, Jenn thought angrily. That thought triggered a wave of fury that raced through her body. Finally, she walked over to where Galadrion was sitting.

"How could you?" she hissed.

Galadrion looked up at her. The pain in her eyes was terrible to see. Jenn's anger began to fade.

"What could she give you that would make you do this?" Jenn demanded.

Galadrion just shook her head and looked back at the floor.

"Freedom," Nakor's voice said weakly from behind her. With a groan, he sat up and looked over at them.

"She offered to remove your curse, didn't she?"

Galadrion just held her face in her hands and began to cry harder.

> Your elf-pain is no match for my vampire-pain!

"I don't get it," Jenn complained. "What curse?" Her exasperation was obvious.

Nakor looked at her for a moment before deciding that Jenn had a right to know. Galadrion might be ashamed of it, but Jenn deserved to understand why a friend had betrayed her. He opened his mouth to speak, but was interrupted.

"I'm a vampire," Galadrion hissed. Suddenly she stood up and slammed her fist into a wall. Flakes of stone fell away where she had punched.

Jenn cocked her head in confusion. "So what?"

Galadrion stared at her, wide eyed. "So I can't even go out in the sun without this charm Thomas gave to me!" she shouted, holding the necklace in one hand. "I go around murdering people and drinking their blood, and I can't stop! I can't die, I can't get old, I can't have children." She was sobbing now.

"I've spent twenty-seven years this way. Twenty seven years of hell!"

Her voice got quiet. "I spend my life running from

people who would destroy me. Religions condemn me for what I became. I had no choice."

She sank back down into the corner. "I had no choice," she whispered again. "It could have happened to anyone."

She looked over at Jenn. "It could have happened to you."

Whoo and Pynne were both awake, and sat silently watching as Galadrion began crying again.

"She promised not to kill you," Galadrion said, wiping away the tears. "She said she'd let you all go after she made sure you couldn't use Olatha-shyre against her."

"You were the one spying on us," Nakor said quietly.

Galadrion nodded. "Olara found the bodies of Jaimus and Erik," she said, looking at Jenn. "She came to me that morning while I was out gathering berries. She said if I didn't help, she'd kill you all right then. But she wanted Olatha-shyre."

"Olara was willing to let you live, and she promised to remove my curse. All I had to do was help her get that spell."

Nakor closed his eyes. He had wondered if one of their group might be the spy. Now, his suspicions had been confirmed. "So why are you in here?" he asked.

> But Nakor had kept those suspicions to himself, guarding them so closely that the author hadn't really bothered to mention them.

Galadrion smiled slightly through the tears. "I was the first to wake up and find myself in here. Olara was standing over me."

"Olara said that, as I had murdered her priests, I must suffer the same death as the rest of you."

"That's good," Whoo commented, "It would be unfair for you to suffer a different death than the rest of us."

Nakor winced as he stood up. "I just wish you hadn't hit me so hard," he complained.

Galadrion looked at him. "That was gentle."

"Right," he answered. Then he looked around the small cell.

"So, shall we get out of here?" Nakor asked.

Pynne rolled her eyes. "Actually, I like it here. I was hoping we could move in."

"What about her?" Whoo asked, tilting his head in Galadrion's direction.

Nakor walked over to where Galadrion sat. "She made a mistake," he said, more to Galadrion than to Whoo. "But she's still a friend."

> Sure, she betrayed me and stopped me from destroying an evil goddess and may have damned the world to an eternity of darkness, but who among us hasn't?

He stood and walked over to the door. "Anyone who has a problem with that can stay here. Besides," he added with a grin, "I'm not too happy about the idea of taking on all those priests without her."

Nakor began to cast a spell that would reanimate the door, breaking it free from its hinges. Then he frowned. As he focussed the energy for the spell, it dissipated around him.

"What's the matter?" Pynne asked.

"Cast a spell, would you?" Nakor said.

Pynne shrugged and began her spell. Then she stopped abruptly. "It doesn't work!" she protested, outraged.

"This room absorbs the energy of any spell cast within it," Galadrion said quietly. "Olara was boasting about how she had built it just for Nakor."

Jenn's shoulders slumped in defeat. She couldn't even pick the lock, since it was on the outside of the door. Now it looked like they were all helpless.

"We're going to die, aren't we?" she asked.

Nobody answered.

"Yes, you are," said Olara as she stepped into the room. She didn't bother with the door. Instead, she simply walked through one of the walls to stand before them.

"Nice trick," Nakor commented.

Olara stared at him. "You arrogant little elf. You actually thought this would work, didn't you?" She sounded truly surprised.

"Did you really think it was that simple to destroy me?"

"I had my hopes," Nakor replied.

Olara shook her head sadly. "You die tonight, Nakor. True, I can not be the one to destroy you, but I have many who are eager to carry out that task for me."

She turned to leave.

"Don't despair, though," she called to them, "your friends will join you right after they watch the blood drained from your body." Then she was gone.

"What a bitch!" Jenn said angrily.

Nakor grinned. "I noticed," he said dryly.

There was a quiet scratching sound by the window. They looked up.

Flame looked down at them, trying vainly to squeeze between the bars. Upon deciding they were too close together, he started biting at them with his beak.

"Galadrion," Nakor whispered excitedly, "I need you to do me a favor.

With a tug, Galadrion ripped the first bar out of the window. Glancing around, she made sure nobody outside had noticed. Holding the window with one hand, she passed the bar to Whoo, who flew down and set it quietly on the ground. Quickly, she removed the other bars. Then she jumped down off of Nakor's shoulders to land nimbly on the ground.

Awfully nice of Olara to include a window in

> this prison she built just for Nakor. Doubly nice
> for her to build it somewhere that nobody would
> notice them RIPPING THE BARS OUT OF
> SAID WINDOW.

Flame flew into the room and perched happily on one of
the shoulders Galadrion had just vacated.

"I can't talk to him in here," Nakor explained, "But you
said the room only stops magic that we cast from inside?"

Galadrion nodded.

"Boost me up."

She lifted him with ease until their earlier positions were
reversed and Nakor stood upon Galadrion's shoulders.

> How tall is this thing? Did Olara build them a
> double-decker prison?

"Even Pynne couldn't fit out that hole," Jenn protested.

Nakor didn't answer. With one hand, he set Flame on
the outside sill of the window. Then, he squeezed one arm
through the small opening. By sacrificing a little skin, he
managed to get his head most of the way through as well.

"Don't drop me," Nakor whispered down. Then, crossing his fingers, he cast a spell.

It was as he had hoped. The spell was one that affected
his eyes and ears, which were beyond the confines of the
wall. Quickly, he whispered instructions to the fire falcon.

Flame clucked quietly and flew away. Groaning, Nakor
wrenched himself free of the window.

Galadrion had to dance back in order to catch him as he
fell.

> Writing should be specific. Don't say she danced
> back. Say she moonwalked.

"Thanks," Nakor whispered.

"So what did you tell him?" Jenn demanded.

"Patience," he replied with a smile. "You'll find out."

Jenn rolled her eyes and sighed melodramatically. "You'll find out," she mimicked.

Nakor just smiled and watched the window.

About a half hour later, Flame returned. He hopped through the window, then came to land before Nakor. Flame was clutching something in either claw, making it difficult to stand.

> Once again, we're left wondering what the bad guys are waiting for. Maybe Olara was in the middle of a game of Monopoly?

Grinning, Nakor leaned over and retrieved the items. As he lifted Flame up to his shoulder, he turned to Whoo.

"I believe these are yours?"

Whoo's grin matched Nakor's own as he took his bow and quiver.

"They obviously hadn't gone back in to get our weapons," Nakor commented.

"So now what?" Jenn asked. "He's only got three arrows in there."

"Now we wait to be sacrificed," Nakor answered.

"What a wonderful plan!" Jenn said. "Why didn't I think of it?"

Closing his eyes, Nakor lay back against the wall to rest. Whoo sat down next to him, concealing his weapon underneath the folds of Nakor's robe.

Hours later, Jenn's stomach rumbled angrily. Nobody had bothered to feed them.

"They could at least spare some bread," Jenn complained.

It had gotten dark outside. They could see the campfires outside when Galadrion lifted someone up to the window.

There was a rattling at the door, as if someone was fumbling with a set of keys.

"Get ready," Nakor whispered, crouching down.

"If there's a priest, get him first," Galadrion said quietly. "Otherwise they'll get the chance to defend themselves."

"We don't want that," Whoo said, nocking an arrow. He placed a second arrow between his teeth, where he'd be able to get at it quickly. Drawing back the string, he waited.

The door opened. Instantly, Nakor was sprinting out of the room.

There were two priests. Obviously expecting some sort of resistance, one of them began to cast a spell at the charging Nakor. Whoo's arrow pierced his chest.

Less than a second later, the other priest jerked back with an arrow in the throat. Nakor shoved past the falling bodies, with only one thing on his mind — cast Olatha-shyre.

Nocking his final arrow, Whoo flew out the door. The others followed closely behind, stepping over the bodies of the two dead priests.

"Nice shots," Pynne commented appreciatively.

In the distance, Olara and her priests stood waiting in front of a huge bonfire. Olara's eyes widened as she saw Nakor and the others.

Stopping, Nakor raised a hand and tried once more to cast Averlon's ancient spell.

"No!" Olara screamed. She sent a brilliant bolt of pure energy ripping through the air at Nakor.

Galadrion leapt in front of it, bringing her arms up to shield her face. A detached part of Nakor's mind noticed as she was hurled through the air to land behind him. Then he finished the spell.

Nothing happened. Olara looked around warily, and began to laugh. Nakor looked back at the others. Galadrion lay motionless on the ground. Her chest was smoking from the blast. After a minute, she blinked her eyes.

"Olara couldn't kill me," Nakor said as he knelt down next to her. "Otherwise that blast would have had enough power to rip through both of us."

Priests came running up to surround them. Nobody resisted. Olatha-shyre had failed.

Their hands were tied behind them, and together they walked over to where Olara waited. Even Galadrion was dragged along the ground, still unable to move.

There was a semi-circle of thick, black poles driven into the ground. Many were occupied by prisoners, trapped with their hands tied behind the pole. Nakor recognized Lenora among them.

"Thank you," she whispered as they passed. Nakor glanced back.

"Our children were able to escape safely," she said with a smile.

"Where's Robert?" Nakor asked.

Lenora's eyes fell. "He died, along with four of the others."

Pynne, Whoo, Jenn, and even Galadrion were hauled up and tied to four of the poles. The pixies even had their wings tied together, to prevent them from trying to fly away. Galadrion just slumped to the ground, too weak to stand. Her bonds kept her from falling flat, and she hung awkwardly with her hands behind her back.

Two priests dragged Nakor into the center of the circle, then stepped away. Nakor watched as Olara stepped forward.

"All of you will die, tonight," she intoned. Her voice was low, almost chant-like. "But first we shall witness the death of this man, Nakor."

She looked around at the prisoners. "He who helped resurrect me."

Lenora and the others stared in surprise. Their expressions ranged from anger to confusion.

"You?" Lenora asked, her face a mask of shock.

Nakor nodded silently.

Olara drew her dagger from a sheath at her belt. Holding it up to the light, she displayed it for everyone to see.

The blade gleamed with a brilliant blackness, reflecting the light of the fire.

> You don't usually see a blackness that bright...

A priest stepped forward.

"Lawrence," began Olara, "As the new high priest of Olara, you shall have the honor of carrying out this execution."

The priest bowed, then reverently reached out to take the dagger from Olara's hand.

"Be warned," she continued, looking at Nakor, "Any magic cast at this gathering shall be as useless as it was in your cell. Is this understood?"

Nakor nodded, resigned to his fate.

Lawrence stepped forward. Unwilling to take the chance of getting too close, he grasped the dagger in a throwing position. Then, without any ceremony, he hurled it at Nakor's chest.

The magic inherent in the dagger was infallible. It tumbled end over end, unerringly.

Time slowed down to a crawl for Nakor as he watched the knife get closer. He could see the gleam of the fire reflecting in the blade.

Images ran through his mind, as they had when he stood before Averlon. So, he thought to himself, your life really does flash before your eyes.

> Oh, no. Not more flashbacks!

He looked for one last time over at his friends. Galadrion watched, struggling to hold her head erect. Pynne and Whoo both looked on sadly. Jenn had closed her eyes, unwilling to watch Nakor's death.

It was odd, Nakor thought, for he felt no fear. Instead, a kind of exuberance was coming over him. Unbearable excitement flowed through his heart.

The knife was closer now. Nakor could see the intricately carved spider at the base of the blade. The handle was a rough, black material, with a silver sphere as the pommel. It was really quite ugly.

A flash of amusement passed through him as that last thought. The excitement was almost unbearable now, and he felt as though his heart would burst. He looked over at Olara, who stood with an expression of triumph on her face.

> The excitement was unbearable two paragraphs earlier, but now it's only "almost unbearable." Nakor's excitement is erratic and unpredictable!

"Now," whispered a voice in his head. Averlon's voice. Suddenly the excitement vanished, to be replaced by a strange calmness. Nakor looked at the dagger, now mere inches away. With a mental shrug, he reached out and caught it by the handle.

Before anyone could react, he flipped the knife in his hand and threw it at Olara.

As no normal weapon could, the dagger of a god flew through the air and pierced Olara's chest. Her eyes widened, and she screamed in agony. As it had been constructed to do, the knife swiftly drained the blood from her body.

Unable to stop the magic of her own enchantment, Olara the Spider Goddess fell to the ground and died.

Lawrence looked on in horror. Out of the corner of his eye, he noticed Nakor walking over and untying the prisoners. But he paid it no notice.

"Mistress," he whispered, kneeling next to Olara's body. "Olara."

The corpse began to fade away into nothingness. Soon, only empty air remained where Olara's body had fallen. The black dagger fell to the ground.

Nakor untied the pixies, handing Whoo his bow and quiver. Jenn was already free, and busily untying Galadrion.

> There's a perfectly legitimate reason that none of Olara's priests or minions make the slightest effort to stop them from getting free. You see, they'd been — OH MY GOODNESS, WHAT'S THAT OVER THERE?

Her arms released, Galadrion collapsed to the ground. Mustering her strength, she propped herself up by one hand and looked over at Nakor.

"You did it," she whispered.

Pynne and Whoo were racing around to free the other prisoners. Soon they all stood crowded together in the center of Olara's followers.

"Now how do we get out of here?" Jenn asked nervously.

The crowd was murmuring to itself. Angry voices began calling out for Lawrence to avenge the death of Olara.

Lawrence looked up, hearing his name. He glanced over to where Nakor stood with the others. Moving as if in a daze, he grabbed the dagger from the ground in front of him.

"You will die," he cried furiously. He began to run toward Nakor, lifting the knife above his head.

> "You will die from stabbing! Because I will stab you! With this knife! And then nobody will ever know of my pathetic battle banter."

Then he screamed and clutched his hand. The dagger tumbled to the ground ahead of him, to be retrieved by Nakor.

Lawrence clutched his wrist, from which a small arrow protruded. His eyes were wide as he stared at the wound.

> For crying out loud. Does he clutch his hand or
> his wrist? Or does he just sprout a third arm and
> do both?

"I thought you just disarmed people," Pynne said, looking at Whoo.

"I missed," he admitted with a shrug. "Besides, I don't
like him."

"Nakor," Lenora whispered, coming up behind him.
"Look at the other priests."

"I see them," he answered. They would be difficult to
miss. Dozens of priests were coming forward, surrounding
the small group.

The perfect calm that had come over Nakor remained
with him still. He took a step away from the group and
raised his hands.

"No more death," he said in a low voice. "There will be
no more killing tonight."

Lawrence stared at him, forgetting the pain in his wrist.
"Destroy them!" he screamed.

Nakor raised his hands above his head, spreading his fingers.

"I said there shall be no more death tonight," he
shouted.

The priests began casting their spells. Streaks of energy
of every color imaginable shot forward at the group.
Streams of flame and bolts of lightning were launched by
the more gifted priests.

> Remember, they're standing in a circle with
> Nakor et al. in the center, and they're shooting
> all this lethal magic. I think it's safe to say these
> are not the brightest torches in the dungeon.

As the magical attacks flew toward their targets, their
paths were warped. The priests' spells curved around to
avoid the prisoners, slamming into Nakor's upstretched

hands.

Nakor stood without moving, illuminated by the brilliant light of the attack. Redoubling their efforts, the priests sent more spells forth, only to have them redirected as the first had been.

> I don't know exactly what's going on here, but it's a Rule that every fantasy protagonist has to have a Moment of Badass. Regardless of whether or not it makes any sense whatsoever.

Still, Nakor was unharmed. "I said no more," he whispered. His voice was drowned out by the howl of the magic around him. A priest collapsed unconscious. He had been unable to sustain the spell he had cast.

Soon, others followed. A few minutes later, the remaining priests ceased their attack.

Nakor lowered his hands and looked around. Only seven priests still stood, Lawrence included. Behind them, hundreds of others watched in silence.

"Olara is dead," Nakor pronounced.

A spear flew through the air, hurled by one of the onlookers. Nakor gestured, and it slammed into the ground at his feet.

> "Stop that! Weren't you paying attention to my Moment of Badass?"

"It is over," he said, carefully emphasizing every word. Then he looked back at the huddled group of people behind him.

"We're leaving."

Fearfully, the crowd parted before him as he led the others out of the circle. Seeing him leave, a few of the priests sent their magic at the group. But the spells were diverted harmlessly into nearby trees or into the ground.

As they walked, Jenn glanced behind. The crowd was

beginning to disperse. Families walked back to their tents and huts in silence, and began packing their belongings. The few remaining priests were tending to their unconscious companions. Moments later, she watched as the first tent collapsed in on itself. Soon, tents were falling all around, as people readied themselves to return home.

> It's not so much a deus ex machina ending (look it up) as it is a deus ex WTF?

Satisfaction spread through her, and Jenn smiled. Then she turned and followed her friends away from what was once the city of Olara, the Spider Goddess.

EPILOGUE

TWO WEEKS LATER, NAKOR AND THOMAS WALKED together through the forest. Thomas had come to Nakor's home the night before, and they had talked throughout the night. Now, they were journeying back to Thomas's small church.

"Pynne and Whoo returned to their village?" Thomas asked.

Nakor nodded.

"And what of the others?"

With a grin, Nakor told him. "Gavin, the vampire from Olara's temple, caught up with us a few hours after we left. He wanted to stay with Galadrion, and she agreed. They went off on their own two days ago."

"Jenn went with Lenora and the other prisoners. Lenora was one of the people who lost a child to Olara. She was willing to help raise Jenn. Jenn was more than willing to go try her hand at a normal, peaceful childhood."

Children are pretty much interchangeable, right?

He smiled. "I think we gave her enough excitement to last for a lifetime."

"Perhaps," Thomas said with a smile.

Nakor turned to look at him, a serious expression on his face. "Thomas, what happened back there?"

"What do you mean?"

Nakor frowned. "What happened to me? Was it Olatha-shyre?" He looked puzzled. "Lawrence threw Olara's dagger at me, I should be dead now. Even after that, how was I able to protect us from Olara's priests and their magic?"

> It's a nitpick, but I hate comma splices. Two independent clauses? Either make them two sentences, or use a semicolon. Thus ends tonight's punctuation lesson.

Thomas shook his head as they walked. "I don't know, Nakor. I can only assume that after you cast Olatha-shyre, the magic lay dormant until it was needed. From what you say, the spell acted as a conduit."

"I don't understand." Nakor stopped now, to face Thomas.

"Averlon spent weeks in the tunnels, working his magic. For the most part, his efforts had nothing to do with the actual scroll you discovered."

"I retrieved his journal from the temple the day after you returned. It explains that his spell would allow him to transfer his magic forward in time to the user. Olatha-shyre was merely the means for that transfer. The real power came from Averlon's exploration of the greater art of magic."

"So when I heard Averlon's voice in my head," Nakor began, "That was really Averlon speaking to me?" A look of comprehension spread over his face. "Averlon slowed down time to let me catch the dagger."

"I suspect you are correct," Thomas answered. "Of

course, we will probably never know for certain."

"But what happened after that?" Nakor asked. "I was trying to protect my friends, but I knew it would be futile. I don't have the power for that kind of defense."

He looked at Thomas, confused. "But it worked."

Thomas smiled and began walking once more. "You and Averlon were connected for a time. For a brief moment, you shared his knowledge of the greater art. It allowed you to tap into power beyond what you have known before."

"What is this greater art?"

"You ask a difficult question, Nakor." Thomas was silent for a moment as they walked. "The greater art was lost thousands of generations before you were born. We have only scraps, pieces, of records that describe its use."

"As you know, spells are cast through the caster focussing their own energy."

> Are you kidding me? 50,000 words, and *now* I decide to start explaining how magic works in this universe? In the freaking EPILOGUE?

Nakor nodded.

"The greater art allowed one to tap into other sources of power. It allowed the master to transcend the limits of his individual talents and shortcomings. Illusion, elementalism, healing, all schools of magic were one and the same."

He patted Nakor on the back. "You, my friend, are the first one to cast a spell of the greater art in two thousand years."

They were reaching the clearing where Thomas's temple had stood. It was gone. Only a bare field of grass remained where an ancient building had once stood.

"What happened?" Nakor exclaimed, turning to look at Thomas.

"It is time for us to move on, Nakor," he answered. "It is time for me to move on."

"But how? How could an entire building just vanish?

Even your underground library is gone!"

Thomas laughed softly. "Nakor?"

"Yes?"

"You ask too many questions." Thomas turned and began to walk across the clearing.

"Goodbye, Nakor Morelain," he called. Then, in midstep, he vanished.

Nakor stood there for a long while, staring at the point where Thomas had disappeared.

> If Thomas is such a mysterious and powerful figure, why didn't *he* take care of the evil goddess?

The clouds to the east were just beginning to reflect the light of the morning sun. With a shrug, Nakor walked to a nearby tree and began to climb. Once he reached a sufficient height, the settled himself onto a wide branch, leaning against the trunk of the tree.

There, he sat and watched the sunrise, a peaceful smile on his face.

> And thus our story comes full circle, ending where it began: with cheesy imagery. For those of you who've read the entire thing, all I can say is, I got better!

ABOUT THE AUTHOR

JIM C. HINES' FIRST *PUBLISHED* FANTASY NOVEL WAS *Goblin Quest*, the humorous tale of a nearsighted goblin runt and his pet fire-spider. Actor and author Wil Wheaton described the book as "too f***ing cool for words," which is pretty much the Best Blurb Ever. After finishing the goblin trilogy, he went on to write the Princess series of fairy tale retellings, and is currently working on the Magic ex Libris books, a modern-day fantasy series about a magic-wielding librarian, a dryad, a secret society founded by Johannes Gutenberg, a flaming spider, and an enchanted convertible. His short fiction has appeared in more than 50 magazines and anthologies.

Jim is an active blogger about topics ranging from sexism and harassment to zombie-themed Christmas carols, and won the Hugo Award for Best Fan Writer in 2012. He has an undergraduate degree in psychology and a Masters in English, and lives with his wife and two children in mid-Michigan. You can find him online at www.jimchines.com.

CPSIA information can be obtained at www.ICGtesting.com
Printed in the USA
BVOW04s0203020115

381675BV00010B/30/P